I0658037

Fireworks

A TJ JENSEN MYSTERY

IN

PARADISE

**The Tj Jensen Mystery Series
by Kathi Daley**

Praise for the Tj Jensen Mystery Series

"Daley's characters come to life on the page. Her novels are filled with a little mystery and a little romance which makes for a murderous adventure."

– Tonya Kappes,
USA Today Bestselling Author of *Fixin' To Die*

"Daley's mysteries offer as much sizzle and pop as fireworks on a hot summer's day."

– Mary Kennedy,
Author of The Dream Club Mysteries

"I'm a huge fan of Kathi's books. I think I've read every one. Without a doubt, she's a gifted cozy mystery author and I eagerly await each new release!"

– Dianne Harman,
Author of the High Desert Cozy Mysteries

"Intriguing, likeable characters, keep-you-guessing mysteries, and settings that literally transport you to Paradise...Daley's stories draw you in and keep you glued until the very last page."

– Tracy Weber,
Agatha-Nominated Author of the Downward Dog Mysteries

"Daley really knows how to write a top-notch cozy."

– *MJB Reviewers*

"Kathi Daley writes a story with a puzzling cold-case mystery while highlighting...the love of home, family, and good friends."

– *Chatting About Cozies*

Fireworks

A TJ JENSEN MYSTERY

IN
PARADISE

KATHI DALEY

HENERY PRESS

Copyright

FIREWORKS IN PARADISE
A Tj Jensen Mystery
Part of the Henery Press Mystery Collection

First Edition | October 2017

Henery Press, LLC
www.henerypress.com

All rights reserved. No part of this book may be used or
reproduced in any manner whatsoever, including internet usage,
without written permission from Henery Press, LLC, except in
the case of brief quotations embodied in critical articles and
reviews.

Copyright © 2017 by Kathi Daley

This is a work of fiction. Any references to historical events, real
people, or real locales are used fictitiously. Other names,
characters, places, and incidents are the product of the author's
imagination, and any resemblance to actual events or locales or
persons, living or dead, is entirely coincidental.

Trade Paperback ISBN-13: 978-1-63511-255-9
Digital epub ISBN-13: 978-1-63511-256-6
Kindle ISBN-13: 978-1-63511-257-3
Hardcover ISBN-13: 978-1-63511-258-0

Printed in the United States of America

This book is dedicated to Echo,
my friend and furry soulmate, who crossed the rainbow bridge
much too early in life. He is loved and missed, but will live on in
my heart, as well as the fictional world of Paradise Lake.

ACKNOWLEDGMENTS

They say it takes a village, and I have a great one.

I want to thank all my friends who hang out over at my Kathi Daley Books Group page on Facebook. This exceptional group help me not only with promotion but with helpful suggestions and feedback as well.

I want to thank the bloggers who have pretty much adopted me and have helped me to build a fantastic social media presence. There are too many to list, but I want to specifically recognize Karen Owen from *A Cup of Tea and a Cozy Mystery*.

I want to thank my fellow authors who I run to all the time when I don't know how to do something or how to deal with a situation. I have to say that the cozy mystery family is about as close knit a family as you are likely to find anywhere.

I want to thank my event coordinator, Jayme Maness, for the book clubs and Facebook events, Bruce Curran for generously helping me with all my techy questions, Jessica Fisher for help with my ads and graphics, and Peggy Hyndman for help sleuthing out those pesky typos.

I want to thank Randy Ladenheim-Gil for making what I write legible.

I want to thank Art Molinares for welcoming me so enthusiastically to the Henery Press family, and a special thank you to Erin George and the entire editing crew who have been so incredibly awesome and fun to work with.

And last, but certainly not least, I want to thank my super-husband Ken for allowing me time to write by taking care of everything else (and I mean everything).

CHAPTER 1

Thursday, June 29

"The captain has turned on the fasten seat belt sign in preparation for our descent into Reno. Please turn off and store all electronic devices, secure your tray tables, and return your seats to their upright positions. The flight staff will be by to collect any trash you may have. We hope you have enjoyed your flight and will travel with us again. We should be on the ground in twenty minutes."

I glanced at the pretty blonde flight attendant announcing the pre-landing instructions. Normally I felt a sense of happy anticipation as the plane neared my home airport at the foot of the Paradise Mountains, but today I felt empty.

"Ms. Jensen?"

I looked up at the flight attendant standing next to my seat. "Yes, I'm Tj Jensen."

"I have a message for you from the ground support staff."

"Message?"

"Apparently you have a very persuasive boyfriend who has convinced the airline to let you leave the plane ahead of everyone else. There'll be someone to escort you to a car that will take you to your destination. Your luggage will be attended to."

"He's not my boyfriend."

The woman frowned at me.

"Kyle Donovan. The man who made the arrangements. We're just friends."

"Oh. I see." The flight attendant continued to stare at me. I could tell she was curious about my mysterious "friend" who seemed to wield so much power. Kyle wasn't an actor, singer, or politician. He wasn't the sort of man to grace magazine covers or be easily recognized in a crowded restaurant. What he was, though, was handsome and brilliant, sweet and charming, and Richie Rich rich. The perfect combination of attributes for talking people into doing anything, whether it butted up against standard procedures or not.

"Is there anything I can help you with prior to landing?" the flight attendant added.

"No. Thank you. I'm fine."

"Do you have items stored in the overhead compartment we can retrieve for you once we're on the ground?"

"No. In fact, just so you know, I don't have any luggage, so there's no need to worry about retrieving it."

The woman raised one eyebrow before continuing down the aisle to collect the last of the trash from the other passengers. I knew the flight staff had been whispering about me since I'd boarded the plane, and to be honest I didn't blame them. Not only had Kyle somehow managed to procure me a first-class seat on a sold-out flight, but he'd convinced the airline to delay takeoff for five minutes so I could make the flight in the first place. Kyle was a simple guy who tended to live well below his means, but when it came to a friend in need, he'd demonstrated on more than one occasion a willingness to do whatever it took to make things happen.

"I'm sorry if this inconveniences you," I said to the woman sitting next to me. We'd just shared a five-hour flight, and other than a cursory hello when I boarded, those were the first words I had spoken to her.

"I'm sure getting to wherever it is you're going must be an important matter."

"It's my father. He's been in an accident. At the time I boarded the plane the doctors were uncertain whether he'd make it or not."

"Oh, dear. I'm so sorry. No wonder you look as frantic as a deer caught in the headlights. What's your father's name?"

"Mike Jensen." I felt a tear travel down my cheek. "He's supposed to be married in the fall. Now..."

The woman handed me a clean tissue from a package she pulled from her jacket pocket.

I thanked her and once again tried to rein in the emotions that had been threatening to suffocate me for the past twenty-seven hours. I glanced out the window at the miles upon miles of barren desert below as the plane circled to approach the city from the north.

"Best to sit back; it's going to be a bumpy landing," the flight attendant warned us all just before she took her jump seat and fastened her seat belt. She offered me a curious smile as we made our final descent.

Everything happened quickly once the plane was on the ground. An employee from the airline met me at the gate and escorted me to a limo that was waiting to take me home to Paradise Lake. When I slid into the backseat, I was overjoyed to see my best friend, Jenna Elston. She opened her arms and I slipped into them, letting out the flood of tears I had been struggling to control since I'd found out that one friend was dead and my father was clinging to life.

"Have you heard anything?" I eventually asked.

"I spoke to Hunter just as your plane was landing. He said your dad's condition is stable, although he still hasn't regained consciousness."

"Did Hunter think he would? Regain consciousness?"

"He's doing everything in his power to make sure that happens."

I let out a small sigh. Hunter Hanson was my good friend, my ex-boyfriend, and the town doctor. I trusted him with my life. More importantly, I trusted him with my father's life.

"This whole thing seems like a dream." I pulled away from Jenna and leaned back into the seat facing hers. "A very, very bad dream."

"I know, sweetie. I feel like someone punched me in the gut and sucked out all the air around me. I can't begin to imagine how you must feel."

I glanced out the window as the desert gave way to forest. It wouldn't be long before we arrived in Serenity. I found that I both wanted to hurry and delay. I'd been running on adrenaline ever since Kyle had thought to check the messages on his satellite phone while we were camping and searching for buried treasure. Hunter had called to inform him that my father had been in a terrible accident and I needed to return to Paradise Lake as soon as could be arranged. At that point Dad's survival was very uncertain. Kyle and I had gathered the family and friends who were with us and headed back to Gull Island via the boat we'd rented as fast as it could take us. Somehow Kyle had managed to book me onto a flight that was scheduled to take off at just about the same time we estimated we'd arrive in Charleston. I remembered the hug of comfort Kyle had offered as I headed toward Security. He'd promised to handle everything, and deep in my heart I knew he would.

"Are you okay?" Jenna asked.

"Not even a tiny bit."

"I know. I don't even know why I asked. Kyle called me half a dozen times, giving me suggestions on how to best help you deal with the situation. I know he's a good friend and wants to help, but some of the things he said were ridiculous. You and I both know there's nothing I can do or say to make you feel any better."

I offered Jenna a sad half smile. Had it really been just yesterday afternoon that I had kissed Kyle for the first time? It seemed like a lifetime ago. "Kyle is a doer. An organizer. I'm sure it's making him nuts that he can't be here to handle things."

"He does seem a bit frantic."

I looked up and met Jenna's eyes as the driver of the limo turned off the main highway that traversed the mountain and headed toward our small town of Serenity. "I kissed him. And not a brotherly peck on the lips."

Jenna smiled. She'd been convinced for months that Kyle and I were meant for each other. "How was it?"

"Wonderful and terrifying and confusing."

Jenna tilted her head but didn't reply. I knew she was waiting for additional details, but the limo had pulled onto the street where the hospital was located.

"We'll talk about it later," I said as we stopped outside the front entrance.

Jenna took my hand in hers as we entered through the double doors. "Your dad is in intensive care. We'll need a doctor's approval to see him since access to the third floor, where the ICU is located, is limited to hospital staff and cleared visitors. Hunter said to call him when we arrived."

I stood staring at nothing in particular while Jenna made the call. My heart pounded with fear as I waited for the hospital escort who would accompany us to the third floor. I had been trying desperately not to let my imagination get the better of me, intentionally blocking the images of my father clinging to life that had been threatening to destroy my last shred of sanity ever since the moment Kyle had received Hunter's frantic call.

When Hunter personally showed up to escort us upstairs my mind couldn't help but leap to the worst possible conclusion.

"Is he...?" My throat closed with emotion before I could finish the sentence.

Hunter opened his arms and I walked into them. I willed my heartbeat to slow as he hugged me tightly and assured me that my father was very much alive.

"Can I see him?"

Hunter looked uncertain.

"Please. I need to see him with my own eyes."

Hunter took a step back and looked at me seriously. "Okay. But be warned: he's pretty beat up. It's going to be difficult to see him that way. Are you sure you're ready for it?"

I nodded as tears streamed down my face.

Hunter glanced at Jenna. "Maybe you should come with us."

Jenna took my hand in hers in silent agreement. Hunter grabbed my other hand and led me toward the elevator that would take us to the third floor. I felt a momentary wave of nausea and dizziness as the elevator doors closed behind us. Both Hunter and Jenna tightened their grip on my hands as I took in a deep breath and let it out slowly.

I'm not sure how to describe what went through my mind when I walked into my father's room to find monitors of all types beeping and chiming all around him. He was covered by a sheet, so with the exception of one eye, which was swollen shut, and the bandage around his head, most of his injuries were hidden. My first thought was that he was just sleeping, but as I let the reality of the situation sink in I found my legs beginning to give out beneath me.

Oh god.

For the first time it hit me that the man I counted on to be there for me more than anyone in my life might actually die.

I couldn't breathe.

Hunter pulled my body toward his and put an arm around my shoulder in support. "Are you okay?"

I took several deep breaths as the room began to spin.

"Tj?" Hunter asked again.

He put a finger under my chin when I still didn't answer and turned my head ever so gently so I was looking at him. "Maybe you should take a break and come back later."

I shook my head. "No. I want to stay."

Hunter hesitated.

"Please. I need to stay."

"Okay, but only for a minute. You look exhausted. I may not be your doctor, but as *a* doctor, I'm prescribing at least twelve hours of sleep."

"Okay." I walked over to a chair that was positioned next to the bed. I sat down and took several deep breaths. It was terrifying to see my big, strong father looking so small and helpless. I gently took his hand in mine and willed him to open his eyes, to assure me that things were going to be okay.

"It looks like you really got yourself into a pickle this time." I tried for a light tone of voice I was far from feeling. "I know it seems pretty bad, but Hunter is here, and he's assured me you'll be getting VIP treatment during your stay."

I glanced at Hunter, who was watching me but not commenting. Jenna was standing next to him with tears streaming down her cheeks. I searched their faces for a sign of encouragement, but all I saw was sympathy.

I bit down hard on my lip to keep from breaking down completely. I turned back to my father and gave his hand a gentle squeeze. I needed to be strong for him the way he'd always been strong for me. "Hunter says you need your beauty sleep, and now that I've had a look at that eye I can see what he means." I reached out my hand and smoothed my dad's hair away from his eyes. It had gotten longer since I'd been away. "If I'm perfectly honest, I could use some beauty sleep as well. I'm going to go home for a while, but I'll be back. It would be really great if you were awake when I returned."

I closed my eyes and prayed. *Please, God, let him live.*

I stood up, leaned over, and kissed my dad on the forehead. Jenna took a step toward me. She wrapped me in her arms as I sobbed. When I had no tears left to expend, Hunter led Jenna and me to his office.

"Okay, tell me everything." I dug down deep for the strength and courage I knew I'd need to get through this.

"Your dad's injuries are extensive, but other than the head injury, none are life-threatening. He has a couple of broken ribs, a broken leg, multiple cuts and abrasions, and of course the swollen eye. All of this will heal in time. It's the head injury that's causing some concern."

I balled my hands into fists as I forced myself to ask the

next question. "What are his chances of waking up and experiencing a full recovery?"

"Better than they were twenty-four hours ago."

"Okay. That's good, but it doesn't really answer my question." I forced myself to look Hunter in the eye. "I need a number. A percentage."

His face was soft with sympathy. "As of this moment, fifty-fifty."

It felt as if a lead ball had been dropped onto my chest. My heart raced as I struggled to find my breath. "Fifty-fifty?"

Hunter crossed the room. He knelt in front of the chair I was sitting in and took my hands in his. "I promise you I'll stay here until he's out of danger. I'll do everything in my power to return the father you know and love to you."

"Could he—" I choked. I took a deep breath, then continued. "Could he have brain damage?"

"It's a possibility. We won't know until the swelling in his brain decreases."

I glanced at Jenna, who was sitting in the chair next to me. I could see she was struggling to be strong for me, although based on the tears on her face, she was losing the battle just as I was.

"Go home," Hunter encouraged. "Get some sleep. If anything changes I'll call you. I promise."

"Rosalie?" Rosalie was my dad's fiancée. I was surprised she wasn't there.

"I sent her back to the resort to get some rest. She was hesitant to leave, but she said she was needed at the resort in your father's absence."

I realized the Fourth of July crowd would be arriving over the next day or two. Fourth of July week was the busiest one of the year at Maggie's Hideaway, the lakeside resort my father owned and operated. We had an excellent staff, but Rosalie would need help. Being needed, having something to do, somehow gave me strength.

"Okay. I'll go to the resort. But you'll call me the minute something changes?"

"I promise."

I looked at Jenna, who had managed to get her own emotions under control. "Is your car here?"

"Yeah. It's in the parking garage."

Jenna took my hand and led me out of the building. It was a beautiful sunny day, which seemed incongruent with the darkness in my heart. Fifty percent! Dad had a fifty percent chance of having a full recovery. What that actually meant, I realized, was that he had a fifty percent chance of not recovering.

I began to shiver as Jenna led me into the parking garage. It was covered, which provided shade against the heat of the sun, but it was a warm day, so the garage definitely shouldn't have been chilly. In spite of the fact that it had to be at least seventy degrees, I found I could not control the goosebumps that covered my arms.

"Are you cold?" Jenna asked, concern evident on her face.

"A little."

"I have a sweater in the car," Jenna offered as she pressed the button on the elevator that would take us to the second level of the garage.

I didn't respond.

"Are you okay? You look a little pale."

I did feel dizzy. I supposed it was the shock setting in. I knew the last thing I had time for was a breakdown, so I took a deep breath, smiled at Jenna, and assured her I'd be fine. I focused on the pavement ahead of me as we made our way toward the second row where Jenna had left her car.

I checked my phone, which I'd turned off while I was in the hospital, as soon as I buckled myself into the front passenger seat of Jenna's car. There was a missed call from Kyle. I hit the Return Call button and waited while it rang.

"Hey," he answered at last.

"Hey yourself."

"Did you make it home okay?"

"I'm in Serenity. At the hospital. Jenna is driving me home."

"And your dad?"

I glanced out the window at the passing scenery as Jenna pulled out of the garage and onto the highway. I put my fingers to my lips and pressed hard as if to hold back the cry of anguish demanding to be heard. "Alive," I whispered, as my voice broke with emotion.

Kyle responded in a tone that sounded forced, but I knew he meant to be supportive. "I spoke to Hunter earlier. He seemed to think your dad had a real chance at a full recovery."

"I hope so." I felt my throat close and the dizziness I'd felt before begin to return. "I don't know what I'll do if he dies."

"He won't. He's strong. He'll get through this."

I wanted so badly to believe Kyle. He was a strong man who fought for what was important to him and, in the time I'd known him, had almost always won. Having Kyle and Hunter fighting with me usually gave me the confidence to do whatever it was I needed to do, but right now, in this moment, I felt so alone.

"Listen," Kyle added, "I managed to get your grandpa and the girls on a flight home tomorrow morning. I'll send a car, so you don't need to worry about picking them up at the airport."

"Thank you." Kyle, Grandpa Ben, his best friend, Doc, and my sisters, Ashley and Gracie, had gone to Gull Island off the South Carolina coast with me for the summer, and I'd yet to really consider what it would take to get everyone home two months ahead of schedule.

"Doc and I are going to pack everything up and ship what we can home. Garrett's sister is going to come early to take over the renovations at the resort." Kyle referred to my father's friend, Garrett Hanford, who we'd gone to Gull Island to help after he'd had a stroke. "Once she arrives, Doc and I plan to hire a private jet if we can find someone willing to fly us home along with all the animals."

"And the cars?"

"Doc and I decided it would make the most sense to leave them here for Garrett's sister to sell. I have another car back home just sitting in the garage gathering dust and your car is on its last leg anyway. I'll buy you something new when I get there."

"You don't have to do that. I can buy my own car."

Kyle hesitated before answering. "Whatever you want to do. We can talk about it when I get home."

He sounded hurt, which made me feel bad. I'd snapped at him and all he was trying to do was help. It was just that having him taking care of me made me feel more helpless than I already did.

"We're almost at the resort," I told him. "I should hang up. I'll call you later."

"Okay."

"Tell the girls I love them. Tell them everything is going to be okay."

"I will. I'll talk to you later."

I waited for Kyle to hang up, but I could hear his breath, so I knew he hadn't. I wanted to tell him I loved him and missed him and appreciated everything he was doing to make this easier on me, but in the end, I simply hung up. The conversation reminded me that my feelings for Kyle were complicated, raw and uncertain. I knew I cared for him, but complicated, raw, and uncertain were feelings I couldn't deal with just then.

CHAPTER 2

Rosalie was standing on the front lawn talking to Noah Sawyer, the new operations manager my dad had hired after I'd decided to head to the East Coast for the summer. I had only met him once, but he'd seemed like a nice competent guy. He'd worked at several large resorts around the world before taking the job at Maggie's Hideaway.

Rosalie ended her conversation as soon as Jenna's car pulled into view. She headed toward the circular drive to meet us. Rosalie was the local veterinarian and I'd always gotten along with her, although things had become somewhat awkward after my dad had proposed and she'd moved in with him, making me feel like a third wheel in my own home.

Jenna came to a full stop. I opened the passenger door and stepped into Rosalie's arms. We held each other for a full thirty seconds before I finally took a step back.

"How are you?" I asked.

"Hanging in. Have you seen him?"

"We just came from the hospital."

Rosalie took my arm and turned toward the house. "You poor thing. You must be exhausted. Let's go in and I'll make you something to eat."

"I'm not really hungry."

"I know. My appetite has been nonexistent since the accident, but you need to eat. Maybe just a sandwich?"

I'd meant it when I said I didn't feel like eating, but I could see it was important to Rosalie, so I allowed her to lead me into the kitchen while Jenna followed behind us. In the kitchen, Jenna and I took seats at the counter while Rosalie began assembling sandwiches.

"What exactly happened?" I asked.

Rosalie sat down on a stool across the counter from Jenna and me. "Your father had been to a town council meeting. His car wouldn't start, so Judge Harper volunteered to give him a ride home. The plan was for Mike to leave his car where it was and deal with it in the morning. Mike called to tell me what was going on so I wouldn't worry when he was late. That was the last time I spoke to him."

Judge Harper was a retired judge and currently the acting mayor of Serenity. He'd lived in Serenity since before I was born and was a close friend of the family. My Grandma Maggie was friends with his wife, Veronica, and the couple came to the resort for dinner on a regular basis. Once Maggie passed, the Harpers didn't come around as often, but I knew both my father and my grandfather considered Judge Harper family.

"Do you know how the accident occurred?"

Rosalie glanced at Jenna, who turned and looked directly at me. "Judge Harper's car was tampered with," Jenna said.

"Tampered with?"

"According to Roy Fisher," Jenna said, mentioning the deputy assigned to Serenity, "the brake line had been cut. There was a slow leak. The brakes failed as they made their way along the lake road on the way home."

"There's that one steep hill," Rosalie added. "They went

over the embankment."

"Wait!" I stood up. "Are you saying it wasn't an accident at all? Judge Harper was murdered?"

"Yes, that's what Roy thinks," Jenna answered.

If I had been numb before, I was darn near paralyzed now. It was one thing when I thought a man I liked and respected had died in a horrible accident, but murder? I wasn't sure how to process this new information, so I simply sat back down on the stool.

"Roy believes Judge Harper was the intended victim and your father was simply an innocent bystander," Jenna continued.

"Does he have any suspects?"

"As of the last time I spoke to him, there were a bunch of people he was looking at, but none of them really stood out."

"I need to call him."

"Hunter said you should rest," Jenna reminded me.

"I can rest later. If the person who killed Judge Harper and almost killed my father is walking around free, I intend to hunt them down and make them pay for what they've done." I picked up the sandwich Rosalie had made for me and took one bite. "Thank you for the lunch. I'll be in my room." I turned and looked at Jenna. "And thank you for everything. I'll call you later. Right now, there's a deputy sheriff I need to talk to."

Once I arrived in my bedroom, where I knew I'd have some privacy, I called Roy, but he was tied up. The receptionist promised to have him call me as soon as he was free. I decided to lay down on my bed for just a minute to rest my eyes while I waited. The next thing I knew, it was dark, and my phone, which had been in my hand when I laid down, was on the table next to the bed. When I realized it was turned off, I wanted to be mad at

Rosalie for interfering in something that was clearly none of her business. But then I remembered the tender way she looked at my father when they'd announced their engagement and realized it would be best if I started keeping in mind that she was suffering as much as I was.

"You're awake." Rosalie stated the obvious when I walked down the stairs and entered the living room, where she was sitting quietly staring out the window.

"Yes. I guess I was tired after all."

"Are you feeling better?"

"A little."

"Can I get you something to eat?"

I was about to remind her that I wasn't a baby and could feed myself, but one glance at the look of fear and hopelessness on her face made me pause. "Thank you. I would like that. A sandwich is fine. I'm going to call Roy while you make it, but I'll join you in the kitchen as soon as I finish."

Rosalie smiled at me. She appeared weak and tired, and I felt petty for being so prickly. She had to be going through her own sort of hell.

"And thank you," I added as Rosalie turned to the kitchen. "Thank you for sitting with Dad and taking care of things here at the resort and making me feel welcome now that I'm home."

Rosalie started to say something and then paused. I could see she had a lot on her mind, and in the end she simply asked if I'd prefer turkey or roast beef. I chose turkey, and she turned and headed off to make my dinner.

I took out my phone and dialed.

"Hey, Roy, it's Tj," I greeted when he picked up.

"Tj, I called you earlier, but Rosalie said you were sleeping."

"Yeah, I was. It had been..." I thought about it. "...I don't know, days since I'd slept. I laid down to rest my eyes and I guess I crashed."

"That's understandable."

"I need you to tell me everything. Jenna said it wasn't an accident."

"She's correct. It appears Judge Harper was targeted."

"Do you have any suspects?"

"I have a ton. The problem is that none of them stand out over any of the others."

I stopped to consider the fact that not only was Judge Harper a retired judge who must have made enemies during his time on the bench, but he was the current mayor, who, in the course of running the town, had probably made new enemies in the year he'd served.

"We've had tough cases before," I reminded him. "We can figure this out. We should meet."

"I agree, but I've been warned by Hunter, Jenna, and Rosalie not to put you in a situation where you'll overdo it."

"I'm not a child."

"I realize that. In fact, you're probably the most capable person I've ever known. Still, I don't want to make matters worse by bringing you into this before you're ready."

"I'm ready. Murphy's in an hour?"

"Murphy's in an hour," Roy confirmed.

Murphy's was a popular local hangout. It had been my grandfather's favorite place to grab a cold one since before I was born, and some of my earliest memories were of sitting next to him at the bar, sipping a soda and watching a game on television. Although I had visited Murphy's many times as an adult, the smell of beer mingling with tobacco still created a welcoming feeling as soothing as a warm hug.

I headed to the table Roy had saved as soon as I walked in. "I'm so sorry about your dad," he greeted me.

"Thank you."

"How's he doing?"

I slid onto the barstool across from Roy. "He's doing okay, considering. I called Hunter before I came over. He said nothing has changed since this afternoon, but every hour of stability is a good thing that improves his odds of a full recovery."

"You know I'm pulling for him."

"And I appreciate it. Now tell me what you know."

Roy hesitated. "Are you sure you want to get involved in this one? You already have a lot on your plate worrying about your father, dealing with the resort, and getting your family moved back across the country."

"I'm sure. I not only want to be involved, I *need* to be."

Roy waved the bartender over and ordered us soft drinks before he began. I could see he both did and didn't want my help this time. I was certain he was struggling to make the right decision. Luckily for him, as far as I was concerned, it wasn't his decision to make.

"You should know the sheriff has assigned a new deputy to the Serenity office since you've been gone. She seems like a competent cop, and I really could use the help, but I'm not sure about her opinion regarding the involvement of civilians in open investigations. You might want to tread lightly until we see what her response is."

"What's her name?"

"Kate. Kate Baldwin."

"Okay. I'll tread lightly around Kate. Now what do you

know?"

Roy took a sip of his soda, then leaned forward with his elbows on the table. "When the accident was initially called in, I believed it to be just that: a horrible, tragic accident. After the car was retrieved and the crime scene guys filed their report, I realized I had a bigger problem than the death of one friend and the injury of another. It was evident that the brakes on the judge's car had been tampered with. Your dad was a last-minute passenger, so it seemed clear it was Judge Harper and not your father who was the intended victim. I've spent most of the day identifying and checking out possible suspects. I hate to admit it, but I haven't gotten anywhere. There are just too many variables. Too many people with grudges against the judge, who we know was a fair but opinionated man."

"I assume you didn't find any physical evidence on the car to indicate who might have tampered with it?"

"No. The brake line was sliced to create a slow leak. The crime lab guys didn't find anything that might help identify who would have done it."

I took a sip of my soda as I considered the situation. The only way to approach it was from a structured analytical perspective: make a list of those individuals with means and motive and eliminate them one by one until all we were left with was the guilty party.

"Do you have a list of everyone you've talked to?"

Roy handed me a copy of his list. I looked at the names he'd added and eliminated. It was, as he'd suggested, extensive. I wanted to be with my dad, and Rosalie could use help with the resort, but I needed to find Judge Harper's killer.

"There are too many suspects. We need a plan. A strategy. Randomly working through this list will take forever."

"Do you have something in mind?"

Did I? I wasn't sure. There must be a way to prioritize. I was noodling on an answer when my phone buzzed. It was one of the nurses from the hospital, letting me know that Hunter had requested she call me.

"I have to go," I gasped, tears gathering in the corner of my eye. "It's my dad. He's in cardiac arrest."

"I'll drive you."

I shook my head as I wiped at the tears that threatened to pour down my face. "I have my grandpa's old truck."

"I'll drive you," Roy insisted.

Serenity Community Hospital wasn't all that far from the bar. Hunter had left permission at the desk for me to go up to the ICU, and Roy, as the local deputy, was ushered into the elevator as well. I was intercepted by a nurse the minute the door opened on the third floor.

"Dr. Hanson wants you to wait in the visitors' area."

"I want to see my dad," I insisted as my heart pounded in my chest. I took a deep breath and slowly blew it out as I tried to control my emotions.

"They're working on him right now. There's nothing you can do to help. Please wait as Dr. Hanson instructed."

Roy took my arm and led me to the waiting area before I could argue any further. After we'd been waiting for several minutes, Rosalie got off the elevator and joined us in the waiting area.

"How is he?" Tears were streaming down her face.

I let out a long breath. "I don't know. Hunter is with him now."

Rosalie looked like she might pass out, so I got up from my chair and led her over to a small sofa where we could both sit.

"I know you're scared. I'm scared too. But Dad is strong. He'll pull through."

Rosalie stared at nothing in particular. She didn't respond, but I really didn't blame her. My dad had been in a serious accident. There actually was a very good chance he wouldn't make it, and all the brave speeches in the world wouldn't change that. I sat back and took Rosalie's hand in mine. She squeezed it in return.

"That night," Rosalie whispered, "when I first arrived. Everyone was running around trying to save Mike's life. They tried to comfort me the best they could, but I could see it in their eyes: they didn't believe he was going to make it." Rosalie paused, tears streaming down her face. She was speaking to me, but she was staring off into the distance. "I remember feeling numb. It was as if I was watching the scene from afar, cognizant as to what was going on but not really part of it. I know I must have been scared, but somehow my emotions were frozen in some sort of stasis. It wasn't until Hunter came in and told me that he was stabilized for the time being that I finally broke down and fell to pieces."

"You were in shock." I knew this to be true because in a way that was how I felt at this moment.

Rosalie didn't respond. She seemed to have drifted away in her own thoughts, so I tightened my hand in hers, closed my eyes, and prayed. We remained seated with our own thoughts and fears for what seemed like hours.

Hunter finally came into the room. "He's stable."

"Thank God." Rosalie turned and hugged me so tightly I couldn't breathe.

I hugged her back and then turned to look at Hunter. "What happened?"

"A blood clot. I'm afraid with the extent of his injuries clotting is always a danger. We have him on blood thinners, so I hope we won't have any more problems."

"Can I see him?" Rosalie asked.

"Just for a minute," Hunter answered.

I started to follow, but Hunter grabbed my hand. "Give her a minute."

"He's my father."

"Yes. But he's her life."

I supposed Hunter had a point. Since becoming engaged to my dad, Rosalie had moved her practice and place of residence out to the resort. She had altered almost every aspect of her life to fit into Dad's. If something happened to him, she'd be lost. I would be as well, of course, but I understood what Hunter meant. I sat back down and waited. After ten minutes Hunter motioned for me to follow him. Rosalie had gone down the hall to the chapel, so I had a few minutes alone with Dad.

"Don't you die on me," I insisted as I placed my hand over his. My instinct was to be weak, but I wanted to be strong. "I know you're tired and it's hard to fight, but you aren't done here. You still need to marry Rosalie and walk me down the aisle someday and hold your future grandchild, should there be one. Ashley and Gracie would be lost without you. You're the closest thing to a real father they've ever had. And Grandpa...I know it seems like he's a strong man, but I'm afraid losing his son would kill him. Please, Dad, you have to hang on."

The room fell into silence except for the steady beeping of the heart monitor. I closed my eyes and prayed harder than I'd ever prayed in my life.

This simply couldn't be happening. This shouldn't have been happening. My dad had so much life ahead of him. He couldn't die. *Please, God, don't let him die.*

I wiped at the tears that were streaming down my face when the nurse came to the door and motioned that my time was up. I held up one finger to indicate one more minute, and then I turned back toward Dad.

"I have to go now, but I'll be back. Don't give the nurses any lip," I said, trying for a light tone that I was far from feeling. I leaned over and kissed Dad's cheek before turning and following the nurse back down the hall to the waiting area, where Rosalie was talking to Roy.

"Where's Hunter?" I asked.

"He had to respond to another call. You both should get some rest," Roy said. "Hunter said he'd let you know if there were any changes."

Because Hunter had done just that this evening, I believed he would keep me informed rather than trying to protect me, which made me feel better about going home, although there was a part of me that felt I needed to stay. I glanced at Rosalie, who looked so lost. I knew I needed to be strong for her. Dad loved Rosalie. He would want me to help her through this.

"Are you ready to go home?"

Rosalie nodded.

I looked at Roy. "I'm going to drive her back to the resort. I'll call Murphy to let him know I'll pick up the truck tomorrow."

"I'll grab someone and run it out to the resort for you," Roy offered.

"Thank you. We'll talk tomorrow?"

"Text me when you're ready."

I nodded my assent before taking Rosalie by the arm and leading her out to the car.

CHAPTER 3

Friday, June 30

I hadn't thought I'd be able to get any rest that night, but I fell asleep the moment my head hit the pillow. By the time I woke up the sun was high in the sky. I looked over the side of the bed expecting to see Echo, but when my gaze fell on the empty rug I remembered he was still on Gull Island. Kyle had left several messages the night before that I'd never returned.

I picked up my phone and dialed his number.

"Hey, Tj. I'm glad you called. How's your dad?"

I felt a tear threatening at the corner of my eye, which I wiped away before answering. "I have no idea. Hunter assures me that he's stable, but Dad still hasn't regained consciousness and he had a setback last night that terrified me. I hate seeing him so weak and fragile. I hate that he hasn't woken up, and I hate that when he does wake up he's going to have to deal with not only months and months of recovery but the fact that one of his best friends is dead. It's all just too much."

"I know. I'm doing everything I can to get home."

I sat up and tucked the pillows behind my back. Now that I was talking to Kyle, I realized I found strength in the sound of his voice and never wanted to hang up.

"How are Grandpa and the girls?" I asked.

"They should be almost home."

"Almost home? I thought you couldn't get them on a flight until today."

"I found an earlier flight and they all wanted to go. I had a car pick them up at the airport. They should be home in about thirty minutes. I left a message on your phone, but I guess you haven't had a chance to check it yet."

"I'm sorry. Everything has just been..."

"I know. It's okay."

"It'll be so good to have them home." I glanced in the mirror and realized if I didn't want to scare the girls I needed to take a shower and wash the puffiness from my eyes from last night's crying jag before they saw me. "I should jump in the shower before they get here. I'm a total mess. I don't want to upset them."

"I'm sure you look beautiful as always, but I understand."

"I want to talk to you about your plans for the trip home as well as the investigation into the accident. I'll call you back as soon as everyone gets settled."

"Okay. I'll wait for your call."

"Kyle..."

"Yeah?"

I wanted to tell him what was in my heart, but I wasn't sure I could articulate the emotions I still hadn't had time to fully process. "Nothing. I'll call you in a bit."

*   *   *

I had time to shower and apply some cover-up before Grandpa, Ashley, and Gracie arrived. Ashley and Gracie had moved to the resort to live with my father, grandpa, and me, after our mother died leaving me as guardian of two half-sisters I barely knew. Rosalie volunteered to take Grandpa over to the hospital while I got the girls settled in. They were tired and worried, which made them cranky and agitated, so I jumped at Jenna's offer to take them to her house for a couple of days, where they could hang out with her girls in a less tense and more relaxed environment.

The girls left and I called the hospital. I'd assumed nothing had changed because no one had called, but I needed to stay involved and informed for my own piece of mind. The nurse I spoke to informed me that Dad was still resting comfortably, that his vitals were stable, and that nothing had occurred to indicate that he might wake up soon.

I wanted to spend time with him, but Rosalie and Grandpa were at the hospital should anything change, so I decided to use the free time I suddenly seemed to have to jump into the investigation into Judge Harper's murder. Grandpa was here to help Rosalie with the resort once they got back from the hospital, Jenna had the girls for a few days and would make sure they were okay, and Dad was in Hunter's capable hands. Everyone had a job to do, and mine was to bring the lowlife who had cut the brake lines and caused the judge's car to run off the road to justice.

I thought about calling Roy, but what I really wanted to do was snoop around to see what I could find at Judge Harper's house. I wasn't sure to what degree Roy's hands might be tied with a new deputy in town, so I decided to snoop first and call him afterward. Judge Harper most likely had locked his house before leaving for the town council meeting that evening, but I'd become pretty good at breaking into places meant to keep out intruders and I had nothing to lose by trying. Thankfully, Roy had Grandpa's truck dropped off as promised, so transportation wasn't going to be a problem.

The judge had lived in a lakeside home in the gated community of Lakeshore Estates. I had visited him there on many occasions, so I knew the code to the gate. All I needed to do once I had access to the neighborhood was find my way into his house without anyone calling Roy to report a break-in.

The houses in the community really were estates, with large lots providing a degree of privacy between them. I pulled into Judge Harper's circular drive and parked near the front door. Then I sat in the truck for a moment, remembering the last time I'd been here. Hunter and I had come together to speak to the judge about cold cases we thought might be relevant when we were investigating the murder of another dear friend. I cringed when I recalled that the result of that investigation had been almost as tragic as the murder itself.

Allowing myself to re-experience the feelings of horror I'd felt when I'd realized who the killer was in that instance would do nothing to change that situation or help me with the current one, so I slipped my phone into my pocket, grabbed the backpack with supplies I'd brought with me, and headed to the front door. Although I was certain Judge Harper would have locked his front door, I tried it anyway to confirm that he had. I went around to try the back door, then circled the house looking for open windows. It was summer and must have been warm lately, so the judge might have left a window open to help circulate the air inside.

I soon realized there wasn't an easy way in, so I set about trying to pick the lock on the front door. I was able to unlock the door, but Judge Harper had installed a deadbolt I wasn't able to deal with. I hadn't wanted to call Roy, mostly because I hadn't wanted to put him in a compromising position, but I couldn't find an access point and I didn't want to break a window, so it seemed to be the only option. Chances were Judge Harper had his house key on the same ring as the one for his car, and Roy would have retrieved that after the accident.

"Hey, Tj. I was hoping you'd call."

"Can you talk? Are you alone?"

"Yeah, I can talk."

"I'm at Judge Harper's. I wanted to take a look around inside. Do you have the key?"

"I do, but we've already searched the house and didn't find anything that stood out as being particularly helpful."

I imagined by the use of the term *we*, he was referring to himself and his new partner.

"I happen to know Judge Harper has a wall safe in his office where he kept his most important files. Did you look there?"

"No. I didn't see a wall safe."

"It's behind the bookshelf. Come over and bring the keys. We'll look together."

"I'll be there in fifteen minutes."

I returned to the truck to wait. There wasn't a lot I could do until Roy got there, and I hadn't called Kyle back, so I took out my phone again and dialed his number. After I'd informed him that Grandpa Ben and the girls had arrived and were occupied for the time being, I asked about his plans for coming home with the animals.

"I found a jet that's willing to transport the three dogs and four cats along with Doc and me. Garrett's sister is due to arrive tomorrow. We've already shipped most of our personal belongings home and I found a dealer to sell the cars, so we should be able to come home on Sunday."

"Good. I'll feel better when everyone I love is home where they should be. How's Echo holding up in my absence?"

"He isn't thrilled with the situation, especially since Ben and the girls left, but he's hanging in okay. I know he misses you and I'm sure he'll be happy to get home."

"And I'll be happy to have him here." I paused and glanced out of the truck window. "I'll be happy to have you *all* home."

Kyle let out a long breath before answering. "I hate that you're going through all this without me there to help."

"You are helping," I assured Kyle. There was a lull in the conversation that, for some reason, made me feel nervous. I hated that things with Kyle seemed to have become so awkward. It would be better after he got home and we could talk about that kiss and what it might mean. "I suppose I should hang up. Roy should be here any minute."

"I spoke to Roy this morning. He told me you planned to help investigate. Be careful."

"Aren't I always?"

"Actually, no."

It was true I'd ended up in tricky situations on more than one occasion. "Roy will be working with me, and right now all we're planning to do is look for files in the judge's wall safe. If we find anything I might call you back to have you do the computer thing." Kyle was a wiz on the computer; I'd relied on him on many occasions to hack into whatever database we needed information from.

"Call me either way. I'd like to be kept in the loop."

"I will. Oh, Roy just pulled up. I'll call you after we take a look at Judge Harper's files."

Judge Harper's office was in the center of his home, so it didn't have any exterior walls. His big desk was situated in the middle of the room, which was lined with bookshelves and file cabinets on three of the walls. A large fireplace occupied the fourth wall. I'd never have known about the wall safe where he kept some of his files if it hadn't been for the fact that I'd been sent by my father to retrieve some paperwork a couple of years earlier. Judge Harper had accessed the safe while I was there.

The bookshelf that hid the safe looked as if it was built into the wall, like all the others, but it was actually on runners. Once I slid the structure to the side, I was able to access the safe and the keypad in the wall beside it. The main problem in getting to the files and whatever clues they might contain was figuring out the combination. As with most safes, it could be opened by entering the correct sequence of numbers. Most people used familiar and meaningful numbers when creating their passwords, so all we needed to do was to determine what numbers would be meaningful to Judge Harper.

I stood looking at the pad, trying to remember if I had noticed any of the numbers the judge had entered the night I was there.

"Maybe he used his birthday," Roy suggested. "Or his wedding anniversary?"

"Do you know either of them?"

"No, I can't say I do."

I got out my phone to call Kyle, who accessed internet records that gave us Harper's birthday, his wedding day, the date he became a judge, and the date he retired. We also tried his wife's date of birth and the day she died.

"There are too many possibilities," Roy concluded after we'd tried twenty different number combinations.

"Assuming Judge Harper accessed the safe on a regular basis, maybe you can identify the numbers used by studying the keypad itself," Kyle suggested. "Are any of the keys worn or more soiled than the others?"

I grabbed a flashlight and a magnifying glass from my backpack and studied each number. The keypad was white with black numbers. To the naked eye, none of the keys appeared more worn than any of the others, but when eyed through the magnifying glass, a clear pattern emerged.

"The three, four, five, and six are noticeably more worn than the others," I said. "But that's still a lot of possible combinations."

"Try three, four, five, six, in that order," Kyle told me. "The second most commonly used passcode to one with special meaning is an easy one to remember."

Three, four, five, six worked. The heavy metal door nudged open to reveal a stack of file folders. I removed them and set them on the desk. "Should we look at them here?"

Roy shook his head. "Let's take them to my place. That way we can look at them without worrying about someone figuring out what we're doing."

"We aren't doing anything illegal," I reminded Roy. "You're one of the deputies assigned to investigate Judge Harper's murder, you entered the house with keys you had in your possession, and you located files revealed to you by a source you trust and have worked with on other occasions."

"I realize that, but now I have a partner to consider. I'd like to keep the fact that we're working together just between us for the time being. As I said before, Kate's a good cop and a nice woman, but based on my observations so far, she has very strong opinions that don't seem to leave room for exceptions to any rules. Until we have a chance to really discuss things, I'd prefer we keep our partnership to ourselves."

"Whatever makes you feel most comfortable is fine with me. Since I have you, however, do you think we could make a stop on the way to your house?"

"Stop? Where?"

"The impound lot. I'd like to take a look at Harper's car."

"The crime lab already went through it. There wasn't anything to find."

"The crime scene guys already went through the house and didn't find the files," I pointed out.

Roy let out a breath. "Okay. We can stop by, but we'll need to be quick. Like I said, at this point I prefer that Kate not know we're working together."

"I won't need long. I'll let Kyle know what we're doing and then follow you to the impound lot."

The impound lot was on the outskirts of town. Any vehicle involved in a crime of any nature was brought to the lot for processing and storage. Cars which were parked illegally or had an excess of unpaid parking tickets were brought to the lot as well.

A wave of nausea gripped me when I saw Judge Harper's car. Based on the twisted remains it was a miracle my dad had even survived. Roy must have noticed that I'd gone suddenly pale because he paused after entering the lot, giving me a few minutes to gain control over my emotions, before proceeding to the car.

"We don't have to do this," Roy said softly.

"I know. I want to. I just wasn't expecting so much damage."

Roy took my hand in his and led me around the exterior of the car.

"It looks like the car has been partially dismantled," I said, noticing that the front of the car was sitting on blocks and the wheels and fenders had been removed.

"Like I told you before, the crime scene guys have already been over the car. I doubt there's anything to find."

I glanced at the interior though a broken window. There was so much blood. I hadn't expected that, although I realized I should have. I closed my eyes and took several quick breaths before taking a closer look. The rear seat had been removed and the dash had been partially dismantled. Roy was right. If there had ever been anything to find, the crime scene guys would have found it. I suppose I knew that, but I was still glad I had seen the car for myself.

"Let's go," I finally said. "Maybe we will pick up a lead in the files. I'll follow you to your house."

Once we arrived at Roy's house, he cleared the piles of newspapers and unopened mail from his dining table and spread the files in their place, then poured us both a soda. The folders were from cases that had come through Judge Harper's court. He'd been a judge for a long time and had overseen hundreds of cases. What seemed to connect these particular ones were the subjects of the notes he'd made about them.

Roy and I spent a good hour going over those notes before either of us spoke.

"These all seem to be cases in which Judge Harper thought the jury had gotten it wrong."

"Yeah," Roy agreed. I could tell by the frown on his face that he was still trying to work out the significance of what he was looking at. "In almost all these trials the jury's verdict was that the defendant was not guilty, but, based on his notes, Judge Harper seemed to believe that was the wrong conclusion."

"Can a judge overturn a jury's decision?"

"Not if the jury concluded that the defendant was innocent. If the reverse were true and a jury found the defendant guilty while the presiding judge disagreed, there are steps that can be taken, although it's complicated and doesn't happen very often. While most of the files in the safe are trials in which Harper believed the defendant was guilty but the jury disagreed, there are a few exceptions. In these four instances," Roy handed me those folders, "it appears Judge Harper felt the person was innocent, but there wasn't enough evidence to overturn a jury ruling."

I sat back in my chair and took a minute to consider the situation. While the files we located in Judge Harper's safe may or may not be in any way related to his death, in my mind, there was a better than average chance we'd find our motive from within the files. "Say it is true. Say these files represent trials in which Judge Harper believed a person to be guilty but the jury let them off. Why even investigate? It's not as if Judge Harper could have the person retried for the same crime."

"Not the same crime. A different crime."

I frowned as I tried to work this out in my head. "Harper believed the individuals tried in these files escaped the punishment they deserved. He knew he couldn't have them retried for the same crime, so he was working with law enforcement to have those people arrested for different crimes?"

Roy hesitated. "I don't know if that's definitely the case, but based on a cursory examination of these files I'd say it is. His notes indicate that Judge Harper believed these men and women were guilty of the crimes they were accused of, although they weren't convicted. I don't see anything that specifically indicates that he was working with law enforcement to try to rectify those situations, but there are notes tying those individuals to more recent crimes. Maybe Judge Harper planned to turn the information he'd gathered over to local law enforcement later."

"Why? He wasn't even a practicing judge anymore. Why would he bother?"

Roy shrugged. "I honestly don't know. Maybe he had some legal reason for doing it, or maybe he was simply looking into the matters to satisfy his own curiosity."

"Do you think any of these people should be suspects in Judge Harper's death?" I asked.

Roy shuffled the files, separating them into piles. "Most of these trials happened a long time ago. There are a few corresponding cases that are more recent, though. I suppose we could research those to see if anything pops."

I took my cell phone out of my pocket. I'd told Kyle I'd call him back, so he was probably waiting. If there were cases to be researched I knew that Kyle was the best man for the job. At least from an internet search perspective.

I dialed Kyle's number and he answered on the first ring. The poor guy probably had been sitting by his phone for the past hour. I briefly filled him in on the theory Roy and I had come up with. I then asked if he would have time to perform an internet search of all the cases and individuals mentioned in the files we'd selected as potentially being the most relevant.

"I'd be happy to," Kyle answered. "Do you have a scanner?"

"Yeah, I have one," Roy answered.

"Scan the important pages and email them to me. I'll see what I can find out. While I'm doing that, maybe the two of you should look into potential suspects based on Harper's tenure as mayor. There were several hot-topic issues causing controversy at the last town council meeting I attended."

"Such as?" I asked.

"There were several controversial items on the agenda," Kyle answered, "but one of the more organized protests came from the merchants association. They were up in arms about a sales tax Harper was trying to push through to fund an arts program at the schools."

"No one wants to see increased taxes, but I doubt someone would kill him over an extra half cent on the dollar. Was there anyone who seemed to be leading the protest?" I asked.

"I'm not sure what may have occurred while we were away, but at the last meeting I attended, several individuals from the merchants association spoke about the subject, each from a slightly different angle. As I said, they were organized, and they'd gathered quite a lot of signatures to back up their opinion, which at least suggested that if the idea was placed on a ballot, it would most likely be defeated."

"I suppose the conflict could have escalated, but I'm not seeing a strong enough reason to put anyone on the suspect list. Who else do you have?" I asked.

"There's a developer, Striker Bristow, who's been trying to get a permit for a strip mall," Kyle informed us. "The council was divided, but Harper was very verbal about his lack of support for the project. I'm not sure Bristow would kill the mayor to get his way, but I got the impression he isn't used to taking no for an answer."

"Okay, I'll add him to the list. Anything else?"

"The only other thing that comes to mind is the conflict around the proposal to tear down the old post office," Kyle added after a slight pause. "I'm not saying anyone was necessarily upset enough over the issue to kill Harper, but when money or conservation of the environment or community is involved, it sometimes doesn't take much to send someone over the deep end."

"I'll see what I can find out," I told Kyle. "Let us know if you find anything significant in the files Roy is scanning."

"I'll call you as soon as I've had a chance to look at things."

"I should get back to work," Roy said as soon as we hung up the phone. "If you're going to investigate, keep a low profile and keep me in the loop. And Tj..."

"Yeah?"

"Be careful. I don't want you to end up in the hospital alongside your father."

"I'll be careful," I promised before heading out to Grandpa's truck. Kyle had a good point about council business being a possible motive. He'd missed the last several meetings while we were away, but Grandpa's friend Bookman was on the town council too, so maybe I'd pay him a visit.

CHAPTER 4

Bookman, a.k.a. R. L. Hellerman, was a bestselling author, a town council member, and the fiancé of Jenna's mother, Helen Henderson. He'd been friends with my grandfather, as well as the entire Jensen family, for many years, and I knew I could count on him to help me in any way he could. Bookman lived in a lakeside mansion with Helen, who had moved in with him while I was visiting Gull Island.

"Tj, sweetheart." Helen hugged me after answering the door. "Jenna said you were back. How's your father?"

"The same. I was hoping to speak to Bookman. Is he around?"

"He's in his study, working on his next novel."

I raised an eyebrow. "I thought he'd retired."

"He did." Helen closed the door behind me. "But the reality is that writing is in his blood. He tries to quit in order to pursue other passions, but I doubt he ever will."

I found I had to agree with Helen. Bookman had officially retired at least three times that I knew of. "I need to ask him about something important. Do you think it might be okay to interrupt him?"

"Normally I'd say no, but for you, given the circumstances, I'm sure he'll make an exception. Let's check."

I followed Helen down the long hall paneled with dark wood. If I had to bet, I'd say the décor of the house was about to change dramatically now that Helen, who preferred light and airy spaces, had moved in. Helen owned half of the Antiquery, the antique store and café she shared with Jenna. Jenna ran the restaurant, while Helen dealt with the antiques, though she'd taken a lot of time off since she began dating Bookman. The pair loved to travel, and Jenna had indicated that Helen might give up her share of the Antiquery altogether once she married her wealthy fiancé.

I wasn't sure what that would mean for Jenna, who really depended on her help, but with the promotion Jenna's husband, Dennis, had just received at the fire station, it was conceivable she might sell the Antiquery and move on to something else as well.

Helen knocked once on the hardwood door leading to Bookman's office, then opened it and entered without waiting for a reply. "Tj is here to speak to you," she informed her fiancé.

Bookman, a distinguished-looking man with dark hair peppered with gray, looked up from his computer before standing up and crossing the room. "Tj, I'd heard you were back. How's your dad?"

"The same."

"I went by the hospital and tried to visit with him, but I guess that's reserved for family only in the ICU. I told the nurse at the desk that I was like family, but that wasn't good enough."

"I'm sure Hunter can get you in if you really want to visit, although Dad hasn't regained consciousness, so I doubt he'd even know you were there."

Bookman motioned for me to take a seat on the sofa in front of the floor-to-ceiling fireplace. "Still, I think I'll talk to

Hunter just the same. This whole thing has been such a shock. I can't believe Harold is gone."

I sat down next to Helen, who had decided to join us. She was a huge gossip, and I wished I could speak to Bookman alone, but this was her house now, so it would be rude to try to exclude her. "I understand my father and Judge Harper were at a town council meeting before the accident."

Bookman nodded. "Yes. Your father was there to give a report on the resort's part in the upcoming Fourth of July festivities."

"And his truck wouldn't start, so the judge offered him a ride home," I continued.

"That's what I heard as well; I left before they did, so I can't state that as a fact," Bookman answered. "I've spoken to several other people who were still at the community center when I left. Based on what I've been told, I'm fairly certain your father and Harold were the last to leave at the end of the meeting."

I sat back on the sofa and tucked one leg up under my body. I anticipated a lengthy conversation and figured I might as well make myself comfortable. "I'd like to ask you some questions that relate to the accident, but I need you to promise that what we discuss today will remain between us." I looked directly at Helen. "Do you both agree?"

"Certainly," Bookman answered right away.

I continued to maintain eye contact with Helen.

"That's a given," Helen answered. "You know I'm not one to gossip."

I tried not to roll my eyes. If I wanted to talk to Bookman, I was going to have to trust Helen.

"I spoke to Roy," I began. "He informed me that the crash wasn't an accident at all. The brake line of the car had been sliced and he believes Judge Harper was specifically targeted."

"Oh my." Helen gasped.

"I hate to have my suspicions confirmed, but the possibility of tampering entered my mind when I heard what occurred," Bookman said.

"I'll be investigating the case with Roy, though at this point we'd like to keep that fact to ourselves. He has a new partner he doesn't quite have a feel for yet. The last thing we need is for the sheriff to find out I'm helping Roy and come down on both of us."

Both Bookman and Helen reiterated that our conversation would stay within the office walls.

"Roy and Kyle are looking into some old cases Harper had been digging around in, but it occurred to us that another motive could stem from Judge Harper being the mayor. Kyle indicated that he'd ruffled a few feathers since he'd assumed the position."

Bookman sat back in his chair and paused before answering. "It's true Harold has made a few enemies along the way, but I have a hard time believing anyone would kill him over anything involving the town council. I suppose it could be worth looking into. Is there anything specific you'd like to know?"

"We're thinking that whoever did this had a current beef with him. The fact that the brake line was cut while he was dealing with town business could indicate that the person who did it had a matter under discussion at that very meeting."

Bookman opened a drawer and took out a piece of paper. "This is the agenda for the meeting. Most of it was spent discussing the upcoming holiday celebration. There were a few arguments but nothing major."

"What sort of arguments?" I asked. I'd learned during

earlier investigations never to discount anything.

Bookman paused briefly before answering. "There are a few merchants who'd like to see the parade route altered so it covers all of Main Street, from the bridge on the west end to the park on the east end of town, rather than turning north on Pine after it crosses the midway point. Of course, those merchants who currently are on the parade route but would no longer be if the change is made were just as vocal against the change."

I could see how this could be a hot topic of conversation, but, again, not hot enough to kill someone over. "What else?"

"The pancake breakfast has always been held in the high school cafeteria, but it's under renovation, so we discussed the option of canceling the breakfast this year. Some residents petitioned to hold the breakfast outdoors in the park. The controversy arose when a couple of folks on the planning committee pointed out that if a storm blew in we'd have spent all that money on food but would have nowhere to serve it."

Paradise Lake was in the mountains and known for its funky and unpredictable weather. A random storm was a real possibility. "Were there any serious arguments?" I asked.

"Not about the Fourth of July, although there was a lot of squabbling. I guess the most heated argument of the evening was between a man named Striker Bristow and Harold."

That got my attention. "Kyle mentioned him. He wants to build a strip mall."

"Exactly. At this point I think the council is split. Bristow is promising a lot of jobs for the next two years as phase one and, eventually, phase two of the project gets underway. He's also promising an increased source of revenue for the town in terms of the local sales tax. I would say maybe half of the council members believe the promise of jobs and tax dollars justifies a change in the current ordinance prohibiting this type of construction. On the opposing side, Harold and several other council members have argued that new development already has impacted our small-town feel and should be heavily regulated to prohibit Serenity from turning into just another big city."

"I'm assuming Bristow stands to make a lot of money if the project goes forward?"

"Oh yeah," Bookman answered. "After both phases are complete, he'd be looking at a payday of tens of millions of dollars."

Wow, I thought. "Tens of millions of dollars might be a motive to want your strongest opposition out of the way."

Bookman shrugged. "Maybe. Bristow seems like a snake, although he'd need to be pretty desperate to resort to killing a man, and from what I understand, he's been very successful in the past. I can't imagine this one project is that big a deal for him."

I narrowed my gaze. "Maybe not, but he's staying on my list. Anyone else with a grudge against the judge?"

Bookman paused before answering. "Bristow has been the most vocal in his argument with Harold, but Fred Deerborn spoke at the meeting before last."

I knew who Deerborn was. He'd moved to the Paradise Lake area from a small farming community in Kansas and seemed to have a problem with pretty much everyone he came into contact with. "What's he mad about now?"

"The teen center. I'm not sure if you remember, but it lost its lease a couple of months ago. The new location backs up to Deerborn's property. He claims there's been an increase in vandalism in the area since the teens moved in and he wants the center shut down. Harold looked into it and reports of vandalism in the neighborhood haven't changed in the least since the teens have been there. In addition, Harold interviewed some of the neighbors in the area where the old teen center was, and everyone agreed the teens hadn't caused problems in the five years the center had been there. Based on that, Harold decided Deerborn was just blowing a lot of hot air, the same way he does about almost everything, and he told him so. Deerborn wasn't a happy man when he left that meeting. Though, as I said, that was a couple of weeks ago."

"Maybe he's been letting his beef with the teens fester. He might not have attended the meeting this week, but he'd know the judge would be there."

Bookman admitted it was possible Deerborn could have been at the meeting even though he wasn't on the agenda. The room had been packed and he couldn't remember if he'd noticed him or not.

"Anything else?" I asked.

Bookman squinted, considering my question. "There are always petty arguments, but nothing else really stands out. The town employees recently had their annual evaluations. It seems like there's always grumbling from at least a few of them, but I know no one was fired, so I doubt anyone had a strong reason to be angry with Harold. I suppose there could be disgruntled citizens whose names weren't listed on the agenda, but no one specifically comes to mind. I'll think about it and let you know if anything occurs to me."

"Thanks. I know these leads are long shots, but we need a starting point. Judge Harper's role as mayor seems as good as any."

"I hate to even bring this up given the situation, but do you know if Maggie's Hideaway still plans to hold the Fourth of July events your father has been advertising?" Bookman asked.

I hesitated. "I have no idea. I'll look into it and call you. Grandpa's back now, so he'll probably be overseeing things."

Bookman looked surprised. "I wasn't aware Ben was back. I'll call him. Is Doc back as well?"

"He should be here on Sunday if things go according to plan. He stayed behind to help Kyle deal with the animals and such. Grandpa just got back a few hours ago."

"Please let us know if there's anything we can do to help," Bookman offered.

"Yes," Helen, who had been sitting quietly, seconded him. "Anything at all."

"Thank you. I appreciate the offer, and I just might take you up on it at some point." I glanced at the clock on the wall. "I should get going. I want to stop by the hospital to check in on my dad."

"Please let us know if there's any change," Bookman said as he stood up to escort me out.

When I got to the truck I grabbed a binder I had brought along with me and wrote down the names Striker Bristow and Fred Deerborn. I liked having an actual list in front of me now that I'd gathered a couple of names. Two possible suspects wasn't a lot, but it was a start. Maybe I'd have more names to add after I spoke with Kyle. I decided I'd head to the hospital before I called either Kyle or Roy to give them more time to do their research.

The nurse at the station near the elevators waved me through without my having to stop to explain who I was and why I was there. When I got up to the third floor I was informed that my dad was resting comfortably, although there hadn't been any change from the previous evening. I asked if Hunter was in the hospital and a nurse offered to page him to find out. Then I went into my father's room and sat down on the chair next to the bed. There was no sign of Rosalie or Grandpa, so I assumed they'd driven back to the resort.

"Your eye looks a little better today," I said to Dad as I placed my hand over his. "The purple is much lighter and the swelling has gone down quite a bit."

I glanced at the heart monitor, which was beating steadily. I didn't understand what all the lines and tones meant, but Dad looked peaceful and they seemed steady and strong.

"I guess you know Grandpa and the girls are back. Grandpa is going to help out at the resort until you're able to take over. The big weekend is coming up, you know. I should sit down with Noah to figure out what needs to be done."

I paused as I watched the ventilator fill my dad's lungs with oxygen. The setup looked pretty uncomfortable. I wondered if he could feel pain given his state of unconsciousness. I hoped not.

"Ashley and Gracie are with Jenna. I miss them, but I think that's best. They can relax and have fun with Kristi and Kari instead of having to deal with all the stress at home." I looked around the room. "I just went to see Helen and Bookman. They asked about you."

I sat back in the chair for a moment, then leaned forward again. It felt awkward talking to someone who couldn't respond. I doubted Dad could actually hear me, but I'd read accounts of coma victims coming to and reporting they'd heard everything those around them had been saying.

I continued to ramble on, just in case. "Kyle and Doc are still in South Carolina, but they'll be home in a couple of days.

Kyle decided to try to sell the cars rather than driving them back. At first I was irritated that he'd made the decision without checking with me, but then I realized he was just trying to get home sooner, and I really do need a new car anyway. We both know my old one was on its last legs. I need a four-wheel drive, of course, but I'm thinking about trying something new. I liked my Toyota, but maybe I'll look for a Ford or even a Nissan this time. I guess I can go to Reno to look around at what's available once things calm down, although I'm really not looking forward to car shopping. In the meantime, I'm driving Grandpa's truck. I didn't notice your truck in the drive. I should check with Rosalie to see what happened to it."

I glanced out the window, which overlooked the hospital lawn and walkways. It was such a nice day. On any other summer day I'd be on the lake or at the beach, but any other day seemed like nothing more than a distant memory. I got up and walked over to the window for a better view. The sky was painted with white fluffy clouds that looked like they'd been strategically placed against a field of blue.

"It really is a beautiful day," I murmured as I looked down at a flower garden on my right. "Maybe you should wake up and take a look."

I turned around and looked at my father, lying in the bed. Of course he hadn't answered me, but for an instant I thought I'd seen the hand I'd been holding move. Probably just wishful thinking, but I returned to the bed and sat back down on the chair.

"Dad? Can you hear me?"

I stared at his hand, but it was perfectly still. If the power of my will could cause Dad to awaken, I'd sit here all day, but I knew in my heart that he'd return to me when he was ready, so I kissed his cheek and headed out to tackle the tasks I knew the day would bring.

After I left the hospital I decided to call Grandpa and check on the plans for the holiday weekend. I knew our guests were expecting the usual events even if the family was dealing with a personal crisis. "Is Grandpa there?"

"Yes. He's lying down now."

"I think the three of us should talk to Noah and maybe a couple of the other managers. Bookman asked me about the weekend festivities and I didn't know what to tell him."

"The fact that the resort is filled to capacity and our guests are expecting things to go on as planned has been weighing on my mind," Rosalie admitted. "I'm new to this. I have no idea what to do or even where to start."

"Don't worry. Grandpa and I are old pros. We'll help make sure everything goes off without a hitch. I'll be home in thirty minutes. Find Noah and ask him to come over to the house in an hour or so."

I called Kyle to check in after I completed my call with Rosalie.

"Perfect timing," he said. "I was just about to call you."

"You were? Do you have information for me concerning the files?"

"Yes, but I have other news as well. Doc and I are flying home tomorrow morning."

I felt my heart leap, although I wasn't sure if it was a leap of joy or terror. I couldn't wait to see Kyle, but we still had that kiss to talk about, and I wasn't sure exactly where that talk would leave us. "I thought you weren't coming until Sunday."

"Garrett's sister showed up early, so I called the pilot I hired and he had an opening tomorrow. We'll be taking off at around six a.m. our time, so we should be home before noon. I was going to hire a car to pick us up, but with seven animals, I thought maybe we should arrange for a ride."

"You know I'm excited to see you, but we have events at the resort going on all weekend. I'll ask Bookman if he can pick you up."

"I can call him," Kyle offered. "I know you have a lot on your plate right now."

"Okay, thanks. That would help. I have a meeting at the resort. I'll call you back when I'm done and we can discuss the files. I really would like to get this wrapped up before Dad wakes up and realizes what's going on. I want to be able to tell him that the person responsible for landing him in the hospital and killing one of his best friends is behind bars."

CHAPTER 5

By the time I arrived at the resort, Grandpa was up from his nap and Rosalie had set up a meeting with Noah. She'd spoken to Grandpa and they'd decided that it would be best to discuss the situation with Noah and then let him meet with the department managers himself. I hadn't gotten the chance to get to know Noah very well yet, but he seemed smart and capable, and Rosalie was confident he'd be able to carry out whatever decisions we made.

"The resort has been advertising holiday events every day beginning with July first and running through the fourth," Rosalie informed me. "The kickoff for the long weekend is the BBQ cook-off scheduled for tomorrow during the day, followed by a bands-on-the-beach concert in the evening. I feel we're locked into both of them. The contestants for the cook-off are all lined up, as are the judges, with the exception of your father, who planned to serve in that capacity. I spoke to Noah earlier this morning and he didn't see any problem with holding that event as planned. The bands we have scheduled are likewise ready and willing to perform."

"We do this same thing every year," Grandpa confirmed. "I'm sure Noah and the managers can take care of the details in Mike's absence."

"The only thing we'll need to do for tomorrow, then, is to replace him as a judge for the cook-off and announcer for the bands," Rosalie commented.

I glanced at Grandpa. "How about it? You acted as judge for the cook-off for a lot of years."

"Yeah, I'll do it. Let's get Noah to announce the bands, though."

I looked at Rosalie. "What else did Dad have planned?"

"There are various events and competitions for the visitors to participate in on Sunday, including a beach volleyball tournament, a sandcastle-building contest, and a sailboat race. Monday is focused on the finals for the bikini contest at the resort, and, of course, Tuesday is the fourth, with the parade, community picnic, kiddie carnival, and fireworks show in town."

"It all sounds doable to me." I glanced at Grandpa. "Any input?"

Grandpa shook his head. "No. I'll pitch in where needed. The weekend is important to the resort. I wouldn't want to let Mike down."

"Doc and Kyle will be home tomorrow and I know they'll help, and Bookman and Jenna are always willing to pitch in if we need them."

"It'll be good to have everyone home," Rosalie said.

I paused briefly and then changed the subject. "I haven't thought to ask you about the veterinary hospital." Rosalie had moved her practice out to the resort after she and Dad got engaged so she didn't need to travel far should she have patients to attend to. Still, she was probably busy at this time of year and I doubted she had time to fill in at the resort. "Have you managed to cover everything? Is there anything we can do to help?"

Rosalie looked pleased that I'd asked. "I've asked one of my old interns to come to Paradise Lake to help out for a few weeks. I'll need to be on hand during the shot clinics and on call should there be any emergencies requiring surgery, but most of the day-to-day routine is being seen to."

"That's good. What you do is important; I don't want to see your patients suffer."

"Thank you. I appreciate that."

Noah showed up just as Grandpa, Rosalie, and I had made our decisions, and Grandpa took the lead, filling him in on what we'd decided.

"Let's discuss the files one at a time," I suggested later that afternoon as we sat in Roy's kitchen. We had Kyle on speaker on Roy's phone so I could have my phone free if Hunter needed to get ahold of me.

"I found three files I believe deserve our attention," Kyle informed us. "Most of the papers you sent were old and the corresponding notes were dated as well. While it's possible one of the older trials is behind Judge Harper's accident, I doubt it. These three seem to correspond to investigations currently being conducted by either the judge himself or local law enforcement."

"Okay, what do you have?" I asked.

I could hear papers rustling in the background before Kyle answered. "The first is something the judge seemed to be investigating himself; it isn't part of a current investigation by the sheriff's office. It involves a forty-seven-year-old man named Steven Reinhold, who was accused of killing his wife, Jennifer, eight years ago. After a lengthy trial, the jury convicted Reinhold of first-degree murder, even though the evidence was mostly circumstantial. Judge Harper presided over the trial, and at the time he believed the man was guilty, but two months ago he met a woman named Clarissa Halloran. She lived in the same neighborhood as the Reinholds did, and she encouraged him to take another look at the case."

"Do we know why he agreed to do it?"

"She felt that Steven had been set up. While she didn't have proof of this assertion, she did make a compelling enough argument to cause Judge Harper to reconsider his previous opinion. There are a lot of notes to go through and I haven't had the chance to really analyze things, but I think the case is worth our looking into. If Judge Harper had changed his mind and realized Reinhold was innocent, he might also have formed an opinion of who might have been the real murderer."

"Do the notes include any suspects?" I asked.

"There are a lot of names and, like I said, I haven't had a chance to follow up on any of them yet, but it wouldn't be outside the realm of possibility that one of them might have also been guilty of killing a man who'd started to nose around. I'll organize the list and we can start to narrow down the suspect field a bit when I get home."

"That sounds like we have two murders to solve," I pointed out. "Judge Harper's and Mrs. Reinhold's."

Kyle paused and then answered, "I suppose that might be true if, after looking into things further, we come to believe Steven Reinhold really is innocent of killing his wife, as his neighbor believes."

"I have the contact information for the woman who approached Judge Harper in the first place," Roy said. "I'll see if I can meet with her and get some additional information. If nothing else, it'll give us a starting point."

"Sounds good," Kyle responded.

I took out my list and added "Jennifer Reinhold's killer, should Steven be innocent," beneath Striker Bristow and Fred Deerborn in my notebook. "Okay. Who else do you have?" I asked Kyle.

I heard Kyle setting one file aside and accessing another. "A thirty-two-year-old woman named Connie Blake who was accused of three bank robberies that occurred at various places around the lake five years ago. Judge Harper was sure she did it, but the prosecution was unable to come up with compelling enough evidence, so the jury acquitted her. There weren't any additional bank robberies after the trial until four months ago when two banks—one in Indulgence and one in Serenity—were robbed. The MO was similar and Harper suspected Connie was up to her old tricks."

I glanced at Roy. "Can you get your hands on the current incident reports?"

"Yeah, I can get them. I was the one to investigate the bank robbery in Serenity. The Serenity Community Bank was hit just prior to closing. At the time of the robbery there was only one teller on duty, along with the bank manager who was in his office. A single individual dressed in black jeans, a black hooded sweatshirt, and dark sunglasses entered the bank and handed the teller a note demanding that she empty her cash drawer. The teller cooperated and the thief got away with just over three thousand dollars."

"I take it he or she was never caught?"

"That's correct. The bank manager was on the phone at the time and unaware of what had occurred until after the whole thing was over."

"Isn't there usually a security guard in the bank?"

"He'd left early, claiming he was feeling sick to his stomach. The robbery at the bank in Indulgence was similar, and we're operating under the assumption that the same person robbed both banks."

"Did the bank robber pull a gun at any point?" I asked.

"No. It was actually all very quiet. In fact, the bank robber never even spoke, just handed the note to the teller, who turned over the cash in the drawer."

"I wonder why the robber didn't try for more money," I mused.

"He or she probably wanted to get in and out as quickly as possible," Kyle speculated.

"If Connie was guilty, and Judge Harper was looking into it, she would have a motive to want him out of the way," I commented.

Roy agreed, so I wrote her name in my notebook. "You said there were three cases that stood out?"

"The third has to do with domestic abuse and was heard in family court, not by Judge Harper, but he made notes on it, so I decided to point it out. Two years ago Brad Turnball was convicted of beating his girlfriend's four-year-old son, Tommy. He was sentenced to serve time in the state prison and was recently released due to good behavior and overcrowding. Just a month ago, Tommy showed up at school with a broken arm. His teacher didn't buy his story of falling off his bike because he had bruises inconsistent with a fall and reported it to Child Protective Services. Someone from CPS went out to the house and found the boy's mother had renewed her relationship with Turnball. After reviewing the previous case, Turnball was arrested and is in county lockup awaiting trial."

I hated cases in which children were victims and wanted Turnball put away for good this time, but I couldn't see how he could have killed Judge Harper if he was in jail. I interrupted Kyle to say as much.

"It seems Turnball is claiming he's innocent. In fact, he told the arresting officer he was innocent the first time too. He claims it was the boy's mother, Gloria White, who was beating Tommy and he was just the fall guy. On the surface, it seems Turnball is lying. There were no reports of the child being bruised or other evidence of beating while Turnball was in prison, yet as soon as he got out the bruises reappeared."

"It seems obvious the boyfriend is the bad guy," I agreed.

"But Judge Harper wasn't convinced. He was actively looking into some old medical reports he'd found concerning the same woman and another child eight years ago."

"What happened to the other child?" I hated to even ask.

"He was reported missing eleven months before Tommy was born. He was never found and is presumed dead."

I was horrified and had no idea how to respond.

"Did the judge think the mother killed the boy reported missing?" Roy asked.

"He suspected as much."

"Why haven't I heard of that case?" Roy asked.

"Ms. White lived in another state at the time her first son went missing. She currently lives in Indulgence, so the case wouldn't necessarily be on your radar."

I hated everything about this case, but it seemed Judge Harper could have been on to something, so I added Gloria White's name below Connie Blake's and the others'.

"We now have five viable suspects who all appear to have motives for wanting Judge Harper out of the way," I commented. "What should we do next?"

"Track them down, check their whereabouts on the night of the judge's death, and eliminate them one at a time," Roy said. "I'll get started on it right away. Hopefully at the very least I'll have the list whittled down to two or three possibilities by tomorrow."

"There's one other angle I think we should look at," Kyle said. "I realize Judge Harper has been retired for quite a while, but during his years on the bench he was responsible for sending a lot of people to prison. It occurred to me that at least a percentage of those individuals could hold a grudge. I think it might be worth our while to see if any of the convicts Harper sentenced have been released recently."

I glanced at Roy. "You suggested that as well when we spoke earlier."

"I haven't had a chance to look into the possibility that an ex-con has resurfaced, but I'll see what I can find out," Roy answered. "It seems someone with a grudge would act quickly, so I'll see if I can get a list of everyone released from prison in the past couple of months."

"It looks like we have a couple of avenues to investigate." I closed my notebook.

"I've been thinking about Kate," Roy said, referring to his new partner.

"What about her?" I asked.

"I'm going to have to keep her in the loop in terms of this investigation. She'll eventually catch on if I don't. I was thinking about introducing her to the two of you. I don't necessarily need to tell her that we're working together right away, but I think it would be a good idea to at least have you meet her."

"I'll be home by midday tomorrow," Kyle offered. "Maybe

we can have dinner. Somewhere casual like Rob's?"

"Rob's sounds good to me," Roy agreed.

"That would be all right," I agreed, "but we have the concert on the beach tomorrow night, and I may need to be at the resort to help out. I'll call to let you know once I get a feel for how things are going to play out. If nothing else, maybe you can invite her to the resort."

"Sounds even better. We'll chat tomorrow."

CHAPTER 6

"Thank you so much for all your help with the girls," I said to Jenna later that evening as we shared a glass of wine at our favorite bar. "It was a good idea to have them stay at your house for a few days. I was stressed; they were stressed; it was a recipe for disaster."

"I was happy to help. Besides, Kristi and Kari have been miserable since you left for Gull Island. Having everyone back together in the same town again just feels right."

"Well, almost everyone is back," I countered. "Once Kyle and Doc and the animals get home tomorrow it really will feel like things are falling into place. If my dad wakes up, that is. If he doesn't..."

Jenna placed her hand over mine. "He's going to make it."

I tried to smile. "I know."

"Tell me about Kyle and the amazing kiss you didn't want to talk about before."

I felt the heaviness in my heart lighten a bit. "It was pretty amazing. Although..." I frowned.

"Although?" Jenna prompted.

I looked across the table at my best friend. "I've been thinking about it, and I have to admit I find myself wondering if he felt the same way I did."

"Of course he did. He adores you. He has for a long time. I'm sure the kiss was as meaningful for him as it was for you."

"Maybe. Kyle and I have been friends for a long time. In that instant when we kissed on Sanctuary Island it felt like we had turned the corner and become something more. The kiss was one of the most magical moments of my life, but we never had the chance to talk about what, if anything, it meant."

"I agree the timing was unfortunate. If your dad hadn't been in the accident and you hadn't needed to run home, your relationship could have progressed normally. And having to leave things up in the air could leave you both feeling awkward when Kyle gets home." Jenna looked me directly in the eye. "But it doesn't have to stay that way unless you let it. Do you love Kyle?"

"I think so. I mean, yes, of course I love Kyle, but I haven't had the time to process everything, to decide whether I'm *in love* with him. In that moment, under the waterfall, as our hearts and lips met for the first time, I felt sure. But now…"

"You're overthinking things. You tend to do that when it comes to matters of the heart. Love isn't something you have to dissect and analyze. It's something that just *is*."

I sat back on my stool and looked away for a moment before returning Jenna's gaze. "Have you ever wondered what might have happened if you hadn't married Dennis? I mean, you did start dating in junior high."

"Never. I loved Dennis the minute I met him and I've loved him every minute since. Sure, we argue at times, and life can be stressful. But no matter what life brings our way, I know Dennis is the other half of my soul. He isn't only someone I am attracted to and grateful for, but someone I know I couldn't live without." Jenna took my hand in hers. "Look, Tj, you're my best friend and I love you. You're a brave, giving person who I admire and trust with my life. But somewhere along the way you got the idea in your mind that love is something born and fostered. It's not. If you really want to find love—the real kind that's hard and messy, but also beautiful and life sustaining—you're going to have to learn to open your heart and let it in."

"But what if Kyle is regretting the kiss? What if he isn't in love with me?"

"He gave up his life and followed you across the country. Trust me, he's in love with you. The question is, are you in love with him?"

I glanced down at my hand entwined with Jenna's. Even when I'd been dating Hunter again, Kyle had been the one I'd run to when I really needed someone. He'd been there for me every minute of every day since I met him. He was not only a trusted friend but a true partner. But love? I thought about how my heart had raced when he'd kissed me. I remembered the feeling of homecoming I'd felt in his arms.

I knew if I didn't want to risk what I had with Kyle, I needed to figure out what this all meant sooner rather than later.

Rosalie was sitting in the living room staring out the window when I arrived at the resort. She had a distant and contemplative look on her face, but she turned and smiled at me when I came into the room. "How was your night out with Jenna?"

"Good," I answered as I sat down on the chair across from her. "I had a nice time in South Carolina, but it's good to be home."

"And I'm glad to have you home. Your dad and I really missed you all while you were away. Mike mentioned on several occasions that the house was so quiet with everyone gone. Too quiet. I know having me here is a big change for you, and while I love your dad very much and want to be part of his everyday life, the last thing I want to do is disrupt the wonderful multigenerational family you have."

I paused. "I really don't want to disrupt that either, but I thought as a newly engaged couple you would need some space to really settle in. Things, as you know, can be pretty hectic around here when everyone is home."

Rosalie paused before she answered. It appeared as if she was considering her response. "I've been alone for a long time, and I can say without a doubt that quiet is very overrated. Honestly, I'm thrilled to finally be part of a big noisy family. I know your dad wants us all to live here at the resort. I want that as well and hope you'll consider staying now that you are home."

I stopped to look around the room. The resort had been my home for most of my life. I supposed one day I'd marry and move out, but until then it really was the best place for the girls and me. "I'll admit I felt awkward when you first moved in. It isn't that I don't care about you—you know I've always enjoyed our friendship—but change can be hard for me. I do think my time away has given me some perspective, and I know Dad's accident has caused me to look at things differently. So yes, I'd very much like to remain living here for the time being if it really is okay with you."

Rosalie smiled. "It's more than okay."

After we spoke I went up to bed. I knew bringing someone new into what had been so very perfect was going to have difficult moments, but Dad loved Rosalie, and after almost losing him, I wanted nothing more than to ensure he had everything and everyone he needed in his life to make him happy once he woke up.

I was exhausted and should have been able to fall asleep instantly, but I found myself tossing and turning. After trying to force the issue, I finally sat up and turned on the bedside lamp. I grabbed my computer from the nearby table and logged on. If I couldn't sleep I might as well research the suspects we had identified at this point. I knew these things took time, but I had to admit that I felt a certain urgency I couldn't quite explain. Maybe the idea resided in the back of my mind that once the case was solved and Judge Harper's killer had been found, my dad would wake up and things would once again feel safe and normal.

I began by Googling Striker Bristow. In my mind, a man in the pursuit of a payday made the best suspect. The fact that Bristow was a developer with some pretty major projects under his belt made him a public figure of sorts, so I figured there would be a decent amount of information readily accessible. My research turned up some interesting but irrelevant facts. He was born in Atlanta but grew up in Boston. He had degrees in both architecture and engineering and worked for an international developer after graduating college. He set out on his own when he was in his early thirties, and in the eleven years he'd owned his own company he had accumulated an impressive resume of projects. His last project prior to coming to Paradise Lake was a sixty-unit mall in Oklahoma, and before that he developed a ten-unit business complex in Chicago.

I had to wonder why a man with his background even

wanted to mess with a strip mall in Serenity, Nevada. It seemed like a step down from his last project, although Bookman did say the man stood to make tens of millions of dollars.

I tried to find something on Bristow that would support the idea that he was willing to play dirty in order to get what he wanted, but in spite of my efforts I was coming up blank. I did find an article detailing his recent divorce from his second wife. It appeared she had hired a skilled attorney and managed to come away with a fairly significant amount of money. Maybe the strip mall was a way for Bristow to refill his bank account.

After fishing around for another thirty minutes, I decided I wasn't going to be able to dig up any dirt on Bristow, at least not without Kyle's help. I decided to abandon my research into Mr. Bristow at least for the time being and move onto Fred Deerborn. While my Google search for items related to Striker Bristow turned up pages and pages of articles, I only found one item relating to Fred Deerborn: an obituary for his wife dated ten years prior.

I felt a wave of sympathy for the man. I didn't know Deerborn well, but nothing about him suggested to me that he had once been married. He was such a cranky sort of guy that I had a hard time picturing him in a committed relationship with another person. Of course, it could have been the death of his wife that made him an ornery cuss in the first place.

I read the article and discovered Deerborn's wife had been shot and killed during a home invasion, which occurred on the farm the couple lived on prior to Deerborn moving to Serenity. The man who killed Deerborn's wife managed to get away before the police arrived, and, as of the time of the article I was reading, he had never been brought to justice. No wonder Deerborn was so paranoid about the individuals who lived and worked near him.

While both men would remain on my list based on what I'd discovered, I didn't have a strong reason to suspect either one in Judge Harper's death. I made a few notes and then moved onto the names I had listed from the files Roy and I retrieved from Judge Harper's safe.

There wasn't a lot of public information on either Gloria White or Brad Turnball. If Gloria had been involved in Judge Harper's death, it seemed our best bet might be to try to get ahold of police records or perhaps records filed by case workers from CPS. I supposed if we decided there was a link between the child abuse case and Judge Harper's death Roy might be able to get the information we needed, but since my hacking skills were pretty much nonexistent, I doubted there was much more information I could gather that evening.

I felt my energy begin to fade as I attempted to pull up information on Connie Blake. I tried to focus on the screen, but my eyes kept dipping closed. It really was late, and if I wanted to be of use to anyone tomorrow I knew I needed to get some sleep. After a quick look at Blake's Facebook page and Twitter account, I turned off my computer and drifted off to sleep.

CHAPTER 7

Saturday, July 1

The next morning, I decided to head to the hospital first thing. It was going to be a busy day, but I knew I wouldn't be able to focus unless I was able to assure myself that Dad was continuing to improve. Hunter said it would take time for Dad to heal, and I knew I should be patient, but patience was something I really didn't have.

Once I arrived on the third floor, I headed toward the reception desk. The nurse who usually manned the desk appeared to have stepped out and I didn't see anyone else in the area, so I let myself into Dad's room. As I had on my other visits I sat on the chair and took Dad's hand in mine.

"How are you feeling this morning?" I asked conversationally. I really wasn't expecting a response, but it seemed silly to sit there and not speak. "You look a little better today. Your color seems to be improving, and while I'm not a doctor so this isn't an official observation, you seem to be resting easier."

I paused as I looked around the room. It was another beautiful day and it hurt my heart that Dad wasn't awake to enjoy it. I knew that the long days of summer, when the resort was booked to capacity and the campground smelled of smoke from the campfires, was his favorite time of the year.

"I'm not sure if you can hear me or if you are even thinking about things in there, but I wanted to let you know Grandpa and the girls are home. Grandpa was here yesterday and the girls want to come by, but there are age limitations in the ICU. You know, if you would wake up, I could probably arrange for a visit."

I glanced at the heart monitor as it beeped steadily. Nothing had changed since my previous visit, but things weren't any worse. I supposed I should be grateful for that.

"Doc and Kyle will be home later today. I can't believe how fast they managed to get things handled. It'll be good to have everyone back in Paradise Lake. Now all we need is for you to come home and things can once again settle into a normal routine."

I took a deep breath and let it out slowly. This was just so hard. I wanted to believe Dad would be okay, but what if he never woke up? I felt a single tear slide down my cheek. I let go of Dad's hand to wipe it away and when I looked back I swore I saw a finger move.

"Dad? Are you in there?"

Hunter had warned me about involuntary twitches, but I wanted so badly to believe.

"Can you hear the sound of my voice?"

Nothing.

I stared at Dad's hand and willed it to move.

"If you can hear me, Dad, move a finger."

I jumped when his finger moved just a bit.

"Nurse!" I yelled as loud as I could.

The woman who must have returned to the front desk came running. "What is it? Is something wrong?"

"My dad moved his finger. Get Dr. Hanson. If he isn't in the hospital call his cell."

She walked over and took a closer look at the monitor. "Are you sure you saw him move? Sometimes our imaginations play tricks on us."

"I'm sure. Just call Hunter."

The nurse glanced back at the bed.

"Now!" I emphasized.

She turned and left the room. I'd call Hunter myself, but there wasn't any cell reception in this part of the hospital, and I didn't want to leave Dad to go downstairs. Apparently Hunter was in the hospital, because he showed up in the room in less than five minutes.

"You had me paged?" Hunter asked.

"Dad moved his finger."

Hunter approached the bed and looked at the monitor readings.

"I told him to move his finger if he could hear me and he did. Does that mean he's waking up?"

"Maybe," Hunter answered. With one finger, he opened one of Dad's eyelids. Then he shone a light into the eye. "I need to run some tests before I know for sure."

"Did you hear that, Dad? Hunter's going to run some tests. Show him that you can move your finger."

I stared at Dad's hand. It took five or so seconds, but Dad moved his finger once again.

Hunter smiled.

"So he is waking up?" I asked.

"Like I said, I need to run some tests, but yeah, moving a

finger in response to a verbal cue is a very good sign." Hunter looked at his watch. "Even if he is waking up, though, it won't happen immediately. I'm going to order the tests. Why don't you go home? I'll call you when I know more."

I hated to leave just in case Dad did wake up, but Hunter insisted I couldn't stay with him during the tests, which would take several hours at least.

As soon as I returned to Grandpa's truck, I called Rosalie. "Dad moved a finger."

"He did? It wasn't just a twitch?"

"No. It was intentional. I asked him to move a finger if he could hear me and he did. Hunter's running some tests to be sure."

"I should come down."

"Hunter said we can't be with him while the tests are being done. He promised to call us when he knows more."

After I spoke to Rosalie I sat in the truck debating what to do. I wanted to be close by if Dad did wake up, but remaining at the hospital while Hunter performed his tests seemed like a waste of precious time. I considered heading back to the resort when Roy called.

"Hey, Roy, what's up?"

"I hate to bother you so early in the morning, but I have a few updates."

"I want to be bothered. What do you have?"

On his end, I could hear Roy shuffling around. He might have been changing his location or perhaps reaching for notes or paperwork. "After we spoke yesterday I started looking into the whereabouts of the five suspects we identified for the night Judge Harper's brake lines were cut."

"And did they have alibis?"

"I've only managed to track down three of the five so far, and all three have alibis I've been able to verify." Roy cleared his throat. "The car was tampered with while he was parked at the community center for the town council meeting. We know this because Judge Harper was able to drive to the meeting without incident. We also suspect he arrived at the meeting at around five thirty. Two different people have confirmed that he always arrived a half hour early to set up before the six o'clock meeting. The meeting was over at nine thirty and the judge left with your father by ten."

Okay. So far I was following. "So the lines were cut between five thirty and ten."

Roy responded, "We believe whoever cut the line did so closer to ten, probably after it got dark at around nine, but we're using the five thirty to ten window for the time being."

"Okay, so who can we eliminate?"

"Connie Blake was brought in for questioning. She seemed nervous, a lot more nervous than would be expected if she were truly innocent. For a minute I thought we had our killer. It turned out, however, that she was working that night."

I thought for a moment. "I remembered from the file that she works for the electric company. Wouldn't she be off at that time of night?"

"She got a second job working at the café on Fourth Street and didn't get off until eleven. She arrived there at five and her coworkers have verified she never left, so I'm fairly certain she isn't the person we're looking for. I do think she might be behind the bank robberies, though, as Judge Harper suspected."

I crossed the room and sat down on the chair beside the now dormant fireplace. "Why do you say that?"

"For one thing, she seemed super nervous when she was

first brought in, but when I told her we were talking to people regarding Judge Harper's car accident, she relaxed visibly."

I supposed that did make it seem like she might have something to hide. "So she's probably guilty of something, just not tampering with Judge Harper's car. I don't know her well, but I do know who she is. She doesn't seem the type to rob a bank."

"Actually, she does." Roy paused for a moment, then said something to someone before continuing. "Ms. Blake was accused of robbing three banks around the lake five years ago. She was acquitted by a jury, partially, I believe, because the prosecution failed to provide any physical evidence of her guilt and partially because Ms. Blake was a sympathetic character."

"Sympathetic how?"

"Shortly before the first robbery her six-year-old son was diagnosed with a rare form of cancer, and her medical insurance wouldn't cover treatment that was considered experimental at the time. After reading trial transcripts, it seems to me some of the jury believed she was guilty, but, given the reason she seemed to need the money, were sympathetic to her circumstances. Additionally, the bank robber back then, like the one now, took only small amounts of cash from each bank and never showed a gun or was violent in any way."

"So she robbed the banks to pay her medical bills."

"If she's guilty—and that has never been proven, nor has she admitted as much—then yes, that's what it looks like she did. I did some digging and found out that the boy responded to treatment and is doing well to this day."

I couldn't condone Connie Blake robbing banks as a source of income, but in her circumstances, I might have done the same thing. The more I thought about it, the more certain I was that if

Ashley or Gracie needed medical treatment I couldn't afford, I would do anything to get them the help they needed. "If Connie was guilty of robbing the banks back then, why would she start doing it again five years later?"

"Her daughter, who's ten, has diabetes. She needs a kidney transplant and is on the list for a donor. I spoke to some of Ms. Blake's friends who informed me the girl isn't doing well. Ms. Blake is afraid she'll die before her number comes up, so she's looking into private options, all of which are very expensive. It seems to me she got tired of waiting and took matters into her own hands."

I frowned. "What are you going to do? You're not going to arrest her?"

"I can't arrest her; all I have at this point is a theory and absolutely no proof. I do intend to go back to look at the physical evidence we've gathered from the more current bank robberies to see if I can find my proof."

"Roy, she needed the money for her children. Who can blame her?"

"Personally, I wouldn't blame her a bit if she turned out to be guilty, but finding the guilty party after a crime has been committed is my job, regardless of the reason behind it."

I felt terrible for the woman and secretly hoped Roy wouldn't find what he was looking for. "So we can eliminate Connie Blake as a suspect in Judge Harper's death. You said you had three people to eliminate. Who else?"

"Fred Deerborn. It turns out he was at the town council meeting the night the car was tampered with. Initially I considered that he could have snuck out, cut the brake lines, and snuck back in, but the meeting's recorded and Fred Deerborn is visible in the background the whole time. He never left his seat and walked out with a group shortly after it was over."

"And the third person you said could be eliminated?"

"Brad Turnbull is in the county lockup, which we already knew, and couldn't have done it, and based on Judge Harper's file it appears he believed it was the mother and not the boyfriend doling out the abuse. To my mind that gave her motive to want the judge out of the way, but I checked and she was locked up in the drunk tank the evening of the council meeting. She couldn't have killed him, though she might still be the one abusing her son, so I turned the judge's notes over to the prosecutor in the case. He seems to think Harper might have been on to something."

This was a small thing, but it made me feel good that Judge Harper was continuing to help people even after his death.

"Of the initial five, we still have Striker Bristow, who wants to build a strip mall, and someone associated with Steven Reinhold, who's in prison, though Judge Harper believed he might be innocent of killing his wife."

"Correct."

"Did Bristow not have an alibi or did you not speak to him?"

"The latter," Roy confirmed. "I've left several messages for him, but all I'm getting is the runaround from his assistant. I'll keep trying. And Clarissa Halloran, the woman who approached Judge Harper regarding Steve Reinhold's innocence, isn't answering her phone. I'll keep trying to track her down, and I've requested the sheriff's file on the death of Mrs. Reinhold. It might be beneficial for me to familiarize myself with the initial murder investigation as well as the trial file and Harper's notes."

"Sounds like you're doing what you can at this point. Maybe Kyle will be able to help you with the research when he's back."

"There are a lot of notes to weed through and Kyle's help will be appreciated, but Kate is wondering why I've decided to investigate these particular people. She isn't making an issue of it yet, but at some point I'm going to have to tell her the truth about the files we found and the fact I'm working with you."

I narrowed my gaze. "Is Kate working the case as well?"

"She is. So far she's limited her investigation to interviews with the people who attended the town council meeting. They were coming and going all night, and she believes, probably rightfully, that someone must have seen something."

"She has a point. We have the video of the meeting, so we can fairly accurately determine who was there. It makes sense that someone either came or left during the time the car was being tampered with."

"Yes, she does, and she's busy following the idea to its inevitable conclusion, so unless she comes up with something significant I'll just leave her to it. Are we still on for dinner tonight? I'm anxious for you all to meet one another. Bringing Kate into the loop will make my life a lot easier."

I glanced out the window and considered our options. "Why don't you plan to bring her out to the resort? The place is going to be packed, but I'll have some takeout delivered to the house."

"Sounds good. We'll talk later to settle on a time."

CHAPTER 8

After I hung up with Roy, I decided to head over to the Beef and Brew and speak to Hank Hammond. Not only did Hank own the popular lakeside steakhouse, he was also a member of the town council. I figured he might have another take on what, if anything, might have been going on that could have led to Judge Harper's death.

We really only had two suspects: Striker Bristow and Jennifer Reinhold's killer, assuming that wasn't Steven Reinhold. In my mind Jennifer Reinhold's killer was a longshot. Not that I was going to remove them from the suspect list, but it had been eight years and Steven Reinhold's conviction hadn't been overturned. The only conclusion I could come to was that the man had been guilty of the crime he was currently in prison for committing.

As for Striker Bristow, he seemed to make as good a suspect as any, but I felt like he was far from a shoo-in, and at this point in the game we really should open the suspect pool up a bit.

The Beef and Brew didn't open until four, but I knew Hank well enough to know he'd be in the kitchen overseeing the preparation of the soups and desserts that would be served throughout the day. Hank was born and raised on a ranch in East Texas, though he had lived in Serenity for quite some time.

"Well, look what the cat dragged in." Hank greeted me with

a smile on his sharply chiseled face. "I heard you were back."

"I got home on Thursday. I guess you heard about my dad."

Hank lowered his eyes as he stirred something in a pot that smelled like his famous beer-based chili. "I did. How's Mike doing?"

"Better, I think. He may be waking up. Hunter is running some tests."

Hank set his spoon on a plate sitting on the stainless steel counter and turned down the heat to let whatever was in the pot simmer. "That's good news indeed. I still can't believe Harold is gone. To lose your dad as well..." Hank shook his head, then refocused his attention on me. "What can I do for you today?"

"I've been doing my own investigation into the accident that killed Judge Harper and almost killed my dad, and I wanted to ask you a few questions relating to the town council if you have a minute."

"If you don't mind asking your questions while I fill these eclairs, ask away."

I settled onto a barstool while Hank began gathering the ingredients he would need for the creamy filling.

"I'm not sure if you heard that Judge Harper's brakes were tampered with."

Hank looked surprised. "No, I hadn't heard. Who would do such a thing?"

"I'm not sure yet. I know you were at the town council meeting on the night of the accident. I was wondering if anything stood out to you as a possible motive."

Hank paused and looked directly at me. "You think someone who attended the meeting tampered with the car?"

"I think it's a possibility. I know the brakes were tampered with during the meeting."

Hank gathered a couple of items from the walk-in refrigerator and set them on the counter. He appeared to be considering my question as he measured and then dumped the first two ingredients into a large mixing bowl. "There's always a certain amount of bickering that takes place at each meeting," Hank began. "Most of it is just that, bickering. But there have been a few hot topic items as of late. Two come to mind."

I got out my small notebook and a pen, prepared to write down whatever it was that Hank planned to share.

"There's a man named Striker Bristow who wants to build a strip mall."

"His name has come up several times," I confirmed.

"He is a high achiever who isn't used to taking no for an answer. I saw him chatting with Judge Harper during the break we took halfway through the meeting."

"Do you know what they were chatting about?"

Hank shook his head. "No. I honestly didn't pay much attention, but it did appear that emotions were high. There seemed to be a considerable amount of hand gesturing going on and both men had intense looks on their faces. Bristow is close to having enough votes to get the support he needs to move forward with his project. All he really needed to do was get Judge Harper to back off from his aggressive campaign to deny Bristow the permit he needed, and the few remaining holdouts on the council would most likely have gone along with the idea."

"You've been working with Bristow for a while now. Does he seem like the sort to resort to murder to get what he wants?"

"Honestly, no. Bristow is a shrewd businessman, but I don't see him killing a man over a project."

Hank hadn't really told me anything I didn't already know, so I asked him about the second person he had mentioned.

"Duffy Welby."

"And who is Duffy Welby?" I asked.

"He works for the town in the capacity of facilities maintenance. It seems Duffy was tasked with painting the town offices, but for some reason he hadn't followed through with the task assigned to him. Based on what I've heard, Mayor Harper spoke to him about his shabby work ethic on several occasions before coming to the conclusion that it was time to move on. Harper fired Duffy on the very afternoon of his death. Now, I'm not saying the man killed Judge Harper, but I could see him doing something to get back at him."

"Have you mentioned this to Roy?"

"No, but I did mention it to his new partner. She said she'd follow up. I assume she has."

I spoke to Hank for a few more minutes, then headed out to Grandpa's truck. I called Roy, who informed me that Kate had followed up with Duffy Welby, who had a solid alibi. I asked if he had ever gotten ahold of Bristow and he said he was still working on it.

After I left the Beef and Brew, I decided to head back to the hospital. I hadn't heard from Hunter, but I was done waiting. If my dad was going to wake up, I wanted to be there. I hated to think of him coming to and not knowing where he was or what had happened to him. Of course, I knew the nurses were keeping a close eye on him, but when he finally opened his eyes he should have someone he knew there to help him navigate his way back to us.

I pulled into the parking lot and found a space near the entrance. As she had earlier in the day, the woman manning the front desk near the elevator waved me through. When I arrived on the third floor, the nurse who usually worked the desk wasn't there, but I could hear a commotion from down the hall, so it seemed one of the patients needed immediate help. Everyone must have been assisting that one patient; I didn't see anyone else as I walked to my dad's room and let myself in.

As he had been every time I'd come into the room, Dad was lying perfectly still. The ventilator had been removed, but the sound of the heart monitor filled the air as I tried to tame the butterflies in my stomach. I don't know what I expected; I guess I hoped to walk in and find Dad sitting up in bed, chatting with whoever was visiting him. I quelled my disappointment and sat down on the bedside chair. I gently placed my hand over Dad's, but this time he opened his eyes and looked directly at me.

"Tj?"

I was so shocked I just sat there for several seconds before responding.

"Dad?" I started to cry. "You're awake."

"Where am I?"

"You're in the hospital. You were in an accident and have been unconscious for a few days. I need to get Hunter." I stood up and looked around. There were usually nurses lurking just outside the room, but of course when I really needed one there were none to be found. "Don't move," I said as I released Dad's hand. "I'll be right back. I promise. And don't go back to sleep."

I ran for the door and headed down the hall. When I got there, I discovered the man in the room where it seemed the entire third-floor staff had congregated had gone into cardiac arrest.

"You shouldn't be in here," one of the nurses said when I poked my head inside.

"It's my dad, Mike Jensen. He's awake."

"Go and sit with him," a nurse said. "Someone will be there

as soon as we're able to stabilize this man."

I held my breath as I returned to Dad's room, praying I hadn't imagined things, that he'd still be awake. His eyes were closed again and he didn't seem to hear me enter the room.

"Dad?"

I swear my heart stopped in the two seconds it took him to open his eyes.

"How are you feeling?"

Dad narrowed his eyes but didn't answer. He looked dazed and confused.

I sat down in the chair next to the bed and put my hand over his. "It's okay. You don't have to say anything. Hunter's going to be here in a few minutes and he'll explain everything."

"Rosalie?"

"She's at home. I'll call her." I looked toward the door. "As soon as Hunter gets here. She's going to be so happy to see that you're awake."

Dad closed his eyes.

"You aren't going back to sleep? You should stay awake until Hunter gets here."

Dad didn't answer, but he shook his head ever so slightly. He was probably light-headed and dizzy, but I didn't want him to go back to sleep until after Hunter had a chance to examine him and confirm that the danger we'd all been worried about was over. I had no idea whether talking to him would help keep him from falling back into unconsciousness or not, but I needed to do something, so I began to ramble.

"It's a good thing you woke up when you did. Tomorrow is the beginning of the Star-Spangled Spectacular. You worked so hard on the planning for both the resort and the town. I'd hate for you to miss it. Not that I want you to worry about it. Because

I don't. Rosalie, Grandpa, and I met with Noah today and everything is all set. I'm not anticipating any problems."

Dad hadn't responded or even moved since I'd been talking. "Are you still with me?"

"Ice cream."

"You want some ice cream?"

He shook his head ever so slightly. "Cook-off."

"Oh." I realized he'd been listening to my rambling after all. "You want to be sure we ordered the ice cream for the make-your-own-sundae stand we always have at the cook-off. I'm sure Noah has taken care of it, but I'll ask him. Everyone knows you can't have a Fourth of July celebration without ice cream."

Dad squeezed my hand just a bit.

"Grandpa's filling in as judge for the BBQ cook-off and Noah is going to announce the bands. It looks like you lined up a few new ones this year. I think that was a good move. I know everyone has their favorites, but it can't hurt to bring in some new talent." I glanced at Dad. He hadn't moved. "Still with me?"

He nodded but didn't speak.

"Are you dizzy?"

He nodded again.

"I hear our sleeping beauty has decided to wake up." Hunter strutted into the room with a smile on his face and a lightness in his step that hadn't been there the last time I'd seen him.

"Oh, good, you're here. Dad's feeling dizzy."

"That's to be expected. Do you know how long he's been conscious?"

"Not long. I stopped by to check on him and when I sat down and began to talk to him, he opened his eyes."

Hunter reached down and took Dad's pulse. It seemed like

taking a person's pulse was the first thing doctors ever did, even though Dad was hooked up to a heart monitor that should have given him all the information he needed. I supposed going for the pulse must have become a habit for Hunter and other doctors.

Dad opened his eyes and looked at Hunter, who immediately took out his penlight and shone it in each eye.

"Can you wiggle the fingers on your right hand, Mike?" Hunter asked.

Dad did as requested.

"Good. Now how about the left hand?"

Dad complied, as well as moving his right and then his left foot.

"Is he okay?" I asked. "Has the danger passed?"

"Probably. The tests I ran earlier didn't show any sign of permanent damage. I'll run additional tests now that he's awake. As far as I can tell, though, it looks like he's going to be fine."

I looked toward the door. "I need to call Rosalie. She'll want to come here. Grandpa too."

"That's fine, but I'm only going to allow brief visits. Your dad still has a lot of healing to do. We don't want to tire him out."

I took several steps toward the door. Then I stopped, turned around, and looked at Hunter. "Thank you."

He shrugged. "Just doing my job."

"No. It was more than that. I know you slept at the hospital before I got back. Thank you for watching out for him."

"You know how I feel about your dad. He's been like a second father to me. I was happy to do whatever I could to make sure he pulled through. Now go make your call, but remember, short visits."

After I left the hospital I called Rosalie and told her the good news. She had been busy helping out at the resort, so I agreed to come back and help out so she and Grandpa could have a short visit. I wasn't sure exactly what time Kyle and Doc would get here, but I knew if I didn't keep busy I was going to explode with nervous energy.

After I checked in with Grandpa, I headed outside to get an update from the resort managers on the status of the day's activities.

"Tj!" Our guest services manager, Leiani Pope, hugged me. "I heard you were back. How's your dad?"

"Better. He just woke up today, and Hunter thinks he's out of the woods."

Leiani, a native Hawaiian with dark hair, dark eyes, and dark skin, had worked at the resort for years and was more like family than an employee. She was outgoing and personable and a huge hit with the guests who returned year after year.

"I'm so glad. I've been so worried. We all have. It just isn't the same around here without him."

"Noah's been taking the lead in Dad's absence. How do you think he's doing?"

Leiani smiled, her dark eyes shining as she spoke. "Noah's doing great, but I'd say Ben is the one taking the lead. He's been out there since before it got light, making sure everything's perfect."

"Well, he did run this place for a lot of years before Dad took over. If anyone knows what needs to be done, it's him. Do you know where Noah is? I wanted to chat with him about a few things."

"Try the grassy area where they're holding the BBQ cook-off. I saw him there earlier."

"I will, thanks."

I was heading for the grassy area when I saw Bookman's van pull onto the resort road. Bookman had been the one to pick up Kyle, Doc, and the animals from the airport. I changed direction and headed over to the house.

As soon as the van stopped and Doc opened the passenger door, Echo jumped out and ran over to greet me. He was so happy to see me that he almost knocked me down in his enthusiasm. I fell to my knees and wrapped my arms around his neck. My heart filled with joy as I buried my face in his warm clean-smelling fur. Echo licked my cheek as everyone else piled out of the van.

I glanced up and saw Kyle still standing near the now empty vehicle. He was smiling but looked uncertain. I remembered my talk with Jenna. I'd actually thought about it a lot. I knew Kyle cared about me and I cared about him. I didn't want things to be awkward between us, and I knew if we took time to analyze things, awkward really was the most likely outcome.

Making a quick decision, I stood up, told Echo to stay, and ran as fast as I could to Kyle. I jumped into his arms, wrapping my arms around his neck and my legs around his waist. He seemed surprised but managed to catch me without falling over. I looked him in the eye and then leaned forward ever so slowly. I gently and hesitantly kissed him on the lips. His arms tightened around my body, and as my heart raced in anticipation, he pulled me closer and deepened the kiss.

I'm not sure how long we stood there kissing, but at some point Bookman and Doc took the animals into the house. I pulled back slightly and looked Kyle in the eye. "I missed you."

He smiled. "I missed you too."

CHAPTER 9

Bookman had taken Kyle and Doc home so they could retrieve their own vehicles and freshen up after their long flight, but both promised to return for the evening festivities. Jenna came by with all four girls who were now playing in the pool, while I made the rounds to ensure that everyone who had entered the cook-off had everything they needed.

I had to admit I was on an emotional roller coaster that afternoon. I was so happy Kyle was home and hopeful about what the future might hold for us. I was looking forward to tasting all the entries from this year's cook-off and grateful to have a chance to catch up with friends and neighbors I hadn't seen in a while.

"I think my favorite part of the cook-off is the smell," Jenna said as she walked over to join me.

"Hmm," I responded as I stared out at the lake, which was dotted with boats of all types, shapes, and sizes on this sunny summer afternoon.

"I'm sorry Doc couldn't enter his brisket this year. There are always a lot of delicious entries, but his brisket really can't be beat."

"That's nice."

"Are you even listening to me?"

I turned and looked at Jenna. "Of course."

"Somehow I doubt that. Are you thinking about the investigation?"

I grinned. "No. Not that."

"Your dad?"

I put my arms up in the air and twirled around in a circle. "No, not Dad."

Jenna frowned, and then it was as if a light had gone on. "You talked to Kyle."

"I did." I paused. "Actually, talking really wasn't involved."

"Huh?"

I blushed as I thought of the total abandon I'd demonstrated when I greeted him. That really wasn't like me at all. I felt like I wanted to dance on the picnic tables while singing a jolly tune. Not that I would. But I couldn't ever remember being quite this happy. I grabbed both of Jenna's hands in mine as we stood face to face. "We didn't really have the opportunity to talk, but I did take your advice and didn't overthink things. When I saw him, I ran toward him as fast as I could, threw myself in his arms, and kissed him."

"And it wasn't awkward?"

I grinned and shook my head. "Not even a little bit. It was magical. Probably the most perfect moment of my life."

Jenna hugged me. "I'm so glad. You guys are going to be great together. Is he coming back today?"

"Yeah. Bookman took him home to unpack and get his car, but he promised to be back before Roy gets here with Kate."

"Deputy Baldwin, his new partner?"

I nodded. "Roy thought it would be good if we could all meet. It's awkward for him to keep things from her. We're going to have dinner here at the resort. Initially I thought of meeting at the house, but the weather is so perfect I'm thinking maybe we'll have a picnic on the beach. Why don't you join us?"

"I'd like to. Roy's brought her into the restaurant a few times, but we've never had a chance to chat. She seems nice, though."

"He hasn't said much about her. Is she young? Old?"

Jenna paused. "She's about thirty, although she's such a tiny little thing she looks younger. She sort of reminds me of you. She's petite, but she looks strong, and she wears her confidence for all to see. She likely doesn't weigh more than a hundred and ten pounds, but she has a way about her that lets you know she could probably wrestle a mountain lion to the ground."

I had a feeling I was going to like this woman. "I'm excited to meet her. When Roy said his new partner was a woman I guess I was picturing a female version of him."

Jenna laughed. "Not even close."

I looked out over the sea of people gathered to sample the meat from the cook-off after the judging was completed. This event had grown in popularity over the years and the resort now offered shuttle buses from town to deal with the parking issue created by so many visitors. The lawn, as well as the beach, was packed, and based on the number of people wandering around with cups of the resort's signature rum punch in their hand, the bar must be doing a brisk business.

"It looks like Noah's waving me over," I informed Jenna. "He probably wants me to get the judges organized. You can tag along or I can text you when I'm done."

"Text me," Jenna answered, tucking her long blonde hair behind one ear. "I see Frannie over near the ice cream booth. I think I'll go see if the book she was going to order for me ever came in." Frannie Edison was the local librarian.

"I shouldn't be too long. Maybe we can grab a drink before everyone gets here for dinner. I've been running around all day and could use a few minutes to sit down and relax."

"Sounds good."

Most of the cook-off judges had participated during previous years and knew what to do, but there were a few new ones who needed a quick tutorial on how to proceed and what to look for before they began, so I agreed to take on that duty. I was halfway through my spiel when one of the men I knew from a spin class I'd taken a few times interrupted to let me know he had important information he was sure I'd want to hear.

"What's up?" I asked after I had Grandpa come over to finish the introduction to judging speech.

"I heard what happened to the mayor and your dad. I think I might know something you'd be interested in."

"I'm listening."

The man looked around. "Not here. Is there somewhere we can talk in private?"

He was giving me the creeps, and I hated to invite him into the house, so I suggested we take a walk down to the beach. Both the sand and the water were crowded, but the area up under the trees was only sparsely populated. I located a spot away from everyone, then asked him again what he wanted to tell me.

"There's a rumor going around that the mayor was murdered. I don't know if that's true, but if it is you might want to talk to Sam Wilson."

"Sam? Why would Sam kill Judge Harper, or anyone, for that matter?"

The man looked over his shoulder as if he expected

someone to be listening in from behind. Once he was satisfied we were still alone, he proceeded to tell me what I can only describe as a wild and somewhat unbelievable story.

"Not a lot of people know this, but Sam's mother lived next door to the mayor."

I frowned. "Martha Wilson is Sam's mother?" I knew both Sam and Martha, and I knew they shared the same last name, but Wilson is a common name and I'd never put together the fact that they were related. Sam talked about his mother a lot, but I guess he had never mentioned who his mother was.

"If that's the dame who lives next to the mayor, then yes. Anyway, I ran into Sam a couple of weeks ago and we decided to go for a drink. One drink turned into four, and before long we were both spilling secrets best left unspoken. I won't go into a lot of detail other than to tell you the reason Sam was drinking like a fish in the first place was because he was mad at both his mother and the mayor for participating in what he called 'immoral relations.'"

My jaw dropped. "Judge Harper was in a relationship with Martha Wilson?"

"If what he told me was true. Anyway, Sam was more than just a little mad. He was furious. He told me he was going to put a stop to things one way or another."

I paused to think. Judge Harper had been a widower for a lot of years, and I'd been aware that he was close to his next-door neighbor. Martha was a widow close to him in age and they seemed to have similar interests. I knew they were friends— good friends—but lovers? Somehow that didn't seem quite right to me.

"Thank you for telling me this. I'll have a chat with Sam."

"Don't tell him I told you nothin'. Sam is an odd sort of

character, and everyone knows he has a temper. I wouldn't want to find myself on the wrong side of it."

"I won't tell him where I heard about his mother and the judge, and I promise I'll keep your name out of it altogether."

The more I thought about it, the more convinced I was that a son protecting his mother made as good a suspect as anyone. Sam seemed like a nice enough guy, in a dorky sort of way. He was probably in his mid-forties, had never married, and lived alone. I'd had no idea Martha was his mother, but I did remember thinking on several occasions that, based on his personality, his life choices, and the fact that he referred to his mother all the time, he seemed like a man who was a little too attached to his mother. Could he have found out that his mother and the judge were sleeping together and killed the judge due to some sort of outdated moral code?

I decided I needed to talk to Martha before I pursued this idea any further, so I tracked down Jenna and let her know I had to run an errand and would be back in an hour. She was fine with helping Noah should he need it, so I grabbed the keys to Grandpa's truck and took off toward Lakeshore Estates without stopping to speak to anyone else. While the area where Judge Harper and Martha Wilson lived wasn't all that far from the resort, there were a ton of tourists in town for the holiday, causing the traffic through town to move at a snail's pace. By the time I reached Mrs. Wilson's home, a good thirty minutes had passed.

"Tj, do come in," Mrs. Wilson said when I knocked on the door of her large ranch-style home with the neatly painted white shutters. "I've just made some fresh lemonade. Would you care for some?"

"The traffic through town was a bear so I really only have a few minutes. I wanted to speak to you about Judge Harper."

I noticed a look of genuine distress on Mrs. Wilson's face. "How about we sit out on the patio, have a cold drink, and talk? It's such a nice day."

I was hoping for something quicker, but I could see Mrs. Wilson was genuinely upset. I supposed I could text Jenna and let her know I'd be longer than I'd originally predicted. "I guess I have time for a glass of lemonade."

Mrs. Wilson smiled in relief. It occurred to me that she might not have had anyone to talk to about the loss of her friend and neighbor.

"Please do come in." Mrs. Wilson opened the door wider. "The patio is at the back of the house."

I looked around the immaculate house as I walked through. The complementary neutral colors provided a calming effect that I found pleasant. White sofas and armchairs were arranged artfully around a white brick fireplace. Whitewashed pine end tables and a large matching coffee table blended nicely with the light pine hardwood floors. The walls were painted a pale coffee color with contrasting baseboards and molding in a warm chocolate brown.

The color scheme continued out onto the patio with accents of red. Climbing roses trailed up a white lattice, completely covering one entire wall of the soft beige exterior of the house. The brick-red patio, which was a novelty for this area since most sitting areas tended to be wooden decking or cement blocks, was furnished with tan wicker furniture with dark brown cushions.

I sat down on one of the padded patio chairs arranged around a glass-topped table and took a long sip of the cold tart liquid. "I'm here to ask you about something I learned during the course of my investigation into Judge Harper's death."

"You wonder if Sam could have done it," Mrs. Wilson jumped right in. "The new woman deputy wondered that as well."

"She came to speak to you?"

Mrs. Wilson nodded. "I told her there was absolutely no way my Sammy had anything to do with Harold's accident."

"According to what I've been told, Sam believed you were involved in an intimate relationship with the judge."

Mrs. Wilson lowered her eyes. She paused briefly before she answered, "I'm afraid I handled things with Sam rather poorly. He's a good son who looks out for me, but he does have a jealous, possessive side. I suppose that's why I hid my relationship with Harold from him."

"Had it been going on for long?" It really wasn't any of my business, but I gave in to my curiosity.

Mrs. Wilson gazed toward the brick wall that separated her property from his. A look of longing crossed her face before she glanced back toward me. "Harold and I lived next door to each other for more than forty years. The four of us, my husband and me and him and his wife, were close friends for most of that time. After his wife died we no longer went on trips together or spent quite as many weekends in one another's company, but he maintained a relationship with my husband until he passed away eighteen months ago, so I saw him often. When my husband passed, Harold and I began sharing a meal and a card game at the end of the evening. We were both alone and we'd been close friends for so long. At some point our relationship took on an intimate aspect that I knew Sam would never understand, so I hid it from him. A few weeks ago Sam visited me unexpectedly and caught us in a delicate situation. He was so angry. He stormed out of the house, and I didn't see him again until after Harold died in the accident."

I sat back in my chair and considered my response. "Do you know whether Sam ever confronted the judge about your affair?"

Mrs. Wilson nodded. "Harold told me Sam stopped by his place when I wasn't at home. Strong words were exchanged between them. Sam wanted Harold to promise not to see me again and he refused. He told me he tried to reason with Sam, to explain how it was between us, but he wasn't having any of it. Sam has known Harold for most of his life. They were close when Sam was younger. He wouldn't kill him."

I didn't intend to argue with the woman, but I didn't necessarily share her certainty that Sam was innocent. If Kate had been by to speak to Mrs. Wilson, it appeared the fact that she and Judge Harper had been intimate must be known by both deputies. Maybe I'd find a way to slip it into the conversation that evening.

"As long as I'm here and we're discussing Judge Harper's accident, I wondered if you could think of anyone else who might have wanted to hurt him."

Mrs. Wilson frowned. "Harold and I shared intimate details about our lives after we both lost our spouses. I do know there are some members of the community who found fault with decisions he'd made in his roles as judge and mayor. I find it hard to believe anyone would go so far as to kill him because of those disputes."

"I don't disagree with you, but someone slit his car's brake line. Did the judge mention anyone in particular he was having a problem with?"

Mrs. Wilson paused. She narrowed her gaze and tapped a finger against her chin. After a moment she answered, "No. I'm sorry. I can't say that anyone comes to mind."

I thanked Mrs. Wilson for the drink and the conversation and headed back toward the west shore. The traffic was even worse on the return trip, so by the time I finally returned to the resort I had been gone over two hours.

When I saw Kyle's car in the resort driveway my heart rate increased dramatically. Suddenly I felt shy and insecure. When he'd been here earlier in the day I'd acted without thinking, but now that I'd had time to think about things...

I slid out of the driver's side of the truck, then bent over to greet Echo, Pumpkin, and Trooper. Ashley, Gracie, Kristi, and Kari were playing a game of badminton on the lawn in front of the house, while Doc, Helen, and Bookman looked on. I didn't see Jenna, who must still be at the cook-off, and, more importantly, I didn't see Kyle. I was about to approach the group gathered on the lawn when a pair of arms reached out from behind me and pulled me back to a more isolated spot behind the truck.

"I've missed you," Kyle said before spinning me around and kissing me in a burst of pent-up passion. I wrapped my arms around his neck and let my actions be my answer. I felt my heart pound and my entire body begin to tingle as he deepened the kiss. The world fell away as sensation took over for thought. I ran my fingers though Kyle's long blond hair as his arms tightened around me and my body melted into his.

A short time later I took a step back and came up for air. "As nice as this is, we seem to have an audience." I nodded toward the gang on the lawn, who had all stopped to watch the show. "Perhaps we should pick this up later. When we're alone."

"Yeah." Kyle sighed as he fought to control his breathing, which appeared as rapid as my own. "That might be a good idea."

I took one long deep breath and blew it out slowly. I needed to get my head back in the game. Kyle's kiss had taken my imagination to a place which most certainly wasn't appropriate for mixed company. I looked around the immediate area and hoped my thoughts weren't readily evident. "I don't see Jenna. Do you know if she's still helping Noah?"

"She's down on the beach talking to Frannie and Hazel. They have a new theory about who might have tampered with Judge Harper's vehicle. Is that where you were? Tracking down a lead?"

It took a minute for my mind to register and understand what Kyle was referring to. The case. Of course he was asking about where I'd been physically and luckily had no idea where I'd just been mentally. I tried to control it, but I couldn't help but blush. I quickly looked away and glanced at everyone on the lawn. They'd gone back to the girls' game now that Kyle and I were just talking. No one seemed to be paying us the least bit of attention.

Kyle continued when I didn't answer. "They wanted to speak to you, but you weren't here, so they settled for Jenna and me. I came up to the house when I saw your grandfather's truck turn onto the resort road."

I glanced back at Kyle. I fought the urge to pull him into the house so we could finish what we'd started, but I knew that now was not the time, so I decided it was best to change the subject and share what I'd just discovered. "It seems Judge Harper had an intimate relationship with his next-door neighbor, Martha Wilson. Her son, Sam, found out about it and threatened the judge not long before the accident."

Kyle frowned. "Do you think he tampered with Judge

Harper's car?"

I shrugged. "Mrs. Wilson seems certain he'd never do such a thing, but I don't know. The timing is suspect. I don't know Sam well. He's generally a nice if somewhat strange man. It has occurred to me on more than one occasion that he seemed to have a very strong attachment to his mother, although until today I didn't put together the fact that Judge Harper's neighbor was his mother. I just know that Sam talks about his mother a lot."

"I suppose it is nice that the man is close to his mother. Sometimes I wish I was closer to mine. But a son protecting his mother is as good a motive as any to kill someone."

I nodded. "That's what I thought."

Kyle glanced off into the distance. It seemed like he was searching for someone on the beach.

"Are you looking for someone?" I asked.

"Jenna. I think we may need to rescue her."

"Okay, let's go."

Kyle wove his fingers through mine and led me toward the beach. We'd held hands before. Hundreds of times. But this time it felt different.

"Tj," Frannie exclaimed when Kyle and I walked up. "I'm so glad you came to find us."

Hazel Whipple, who was even older and more opinionated than my grandfather, looked intently at my hand entwined with Kyle's but didn't say anything.

I greeted the women, then said, "I hear you have a theory you'd like to share."

Frannie scooted over on the bench to make room for Kyle and me. "We were just explaining our theory to Jenna."

"They really might have something," Jenna offered.

"Okay." I sat down. "I'm all ears."

"Striker Bristow spent a considerable amount of time in the library the day before the accident," Frannie informed me.

"What was he doing?"

"Looking at those same old scrapbooks you asked to see when Zachary died."

The scrapbooks were really a collection of newspaper articles, photos, letters, and other random items from a specific period of time. Each scrapbook covered a couple of years with the oldest one dating back more than two hundred years to the days when Serenity was little more than a lumber mill.

"That does seem odd." Striker Bristow was a businessman in Serenity temporarily while he tried to get a permit to build a strip mall at the edge of town. What would he want with a bunch of old letters and photos?

"That's what I thought, which is why I'm bringing it up."

"Do you have any idea what he was looking for?" I asked.

"Not initially," Frannie answered. "The day he came into the library he asked about historical documents. I pointed him toward some books that discuss the history of the area, but he said he was looking for original documents. I told him I did have some, but he couldn't check them out. I figured that would be that because he appeared to be a busy man. I couldn't imagine he'd want to spend his day sitting in a library."

"But he stayed," Hazel added.

"Did he ask for any specific information?" I wondered.

"No. He seemed interested in a certain span of time—between 1968 and 1978—but he didn't tell me exactly what he was looking for. He did, however, take a lot of notes and quite a few photos with his phone."

I paused to consider what Frannie was telling me. "I'll

admit that does sound is odd, but what would this have to do with Judge Harper?"

"After Bristow left, Harold came in later and asked to look at the same book Bristow had been looking at. He turned to a specific page, read something and frowned, then left. Based on the timing of the visits from the two men, I'm going to assume Bristow found what he was looking for, left to tell Harper, and then Harper came by to verify it for himself."

"Do you know what he was looking at?" I asked.

"No. I've tried to figure it out. I've looked through the book a bunch of times, but I haven't found anything that seems relevant or shocking. There's a chance that whatever Bristow was looking for had significance only to him and Harold. I probably wouldn't have given it much thought once I figured out there was no way for me to identify the page the men were looking at or even if it was the same one, but then Harold was murdered and suddenly the entire thing seemed suspect."

"You may not know which page the men were interested in, but you know which book it was, and you might have seen if it was opened to the front, middle, or end," Kyle pointed out.

"That's true. I do know which book, and I could see they both were looking toward the middle of it, but, like I said, I've gone over every page and nothing stood out." Frannie looked at me. "I thought maybe you could come by to take a look. You seem to have a sense about these things. We're closed on Sundays, but I'll go in tomorrow if you think you might have time."

I glanced at Kyle, who shrugged. "My dad might be moved out of intensive care tomorrow, and if he's moved to a regular room I've made plans to take my sisters to see him. I can come by the library after that. Can I text you with a time once I see how the day is going?"

"Certainly, dear. Any time would be fine. I'm so glad to hear that your dad is doing better. I've been praying for him every day since I heard about the accident."

"Thank you. I'm sure he appreciates all the prayers and good thoughts."

Kyle and I spoke to Frannie and Hazel for a few more minutes, and then Jenna headed back toward the cook-off with the two of us to see how things were progressing.

CHAPTER 10

"Maybe we should check on the girls," Jenna commented as we made our way. "They're fine with Mom and the others, but it's been a while."

"Yeah, about that..." I replied as I walked between Jenna and Kyle. "Kyle and I shared a fairly enthusiastic greeting on the driveway in front of everyone. I'm not sure I'm ready to go back to answer a bunch of questions. So far you're the only one who officially knows about our change in relationship status."

Jenna chuckled. "If what you say is true I think they all know by now."

"Maybe, but I still don't want to talk about it just yet."

Jenna stopped walking and turned toward us. I glanced at Kyle, who didn't look embarrassed in the least by what had happened, but he was wisely letting me do the talking and setting of the pace.

"Look," she said, "it's like ripping off a Band-Aid. Just get it over with."

I grimaced. "I don't know. I never did get the whole Band-Aid-ripping thing."

"It'll be fine. Two minutes of ribbing and you can relax and enjoy the journey."

I didn't answer, but Jenna took my hand and led me toward

the house, Kyle following along behind. When we arrived on the lawn, the girls stopped playing their game. Everyone turned and looked at us.

"So..." Helen began.

"Yes, Kyle and I are together," I blurted out before she could say anything more.

Doc winked at Grandpa, but, thankfully, neither commented. Bookman seemed to be pinching Helen, which shut her up for probably the first time in her life.

Finally it was Gracie, with a look of confusion on her face, who broke the silence. "What does that mean?"

Kyle stepped forward and lifted her in the air. She began to giggle as he replied, "It means nothing will really change except that I'm going to be kissing your sister all the time."

"Eww," eight-year-old Gracie and seven-year-old Kari said in unison.

Ashley and Kristi began giggling and whispering to each other, but it seemed everyone was fine with the situation.

"I need to call Roy," I said, desperately needing a few minutes to myself. "He's bringing his new partner for us to meet. Kyle, Jenna, and I are having dinner with them."

Kyle distracted the girls while I headed for the house and the bathroom, where I splashed cold water on my face. I really had no idea what was wrong with me. I wasn't a kid with her first crush. I'd been in other relationships, but I'd never before felt as nervous about what that would mean as I did now. I stopped in the living room and looked out the window. Kyle had teamed up with Gracie and Kari to play badminton against Jenna, Ashley, and Kristi, and the others were talking among themselves on the sidelines. Everyone looked happy and relaxed. It was ridiculous that I was such a nervous wreck.

Obviously everyone except the four girls had already figured out what was going on between Kyle and me, probably before we had.

I smiled as I continued to watch the scene on the lawn. It really was good to be home.

I took out my phone and called Roy. He didn't pick up, so I left a message. "Hey, Roy, it's Tj. Just checking in about tonight. I know I initially mentioned having some food sent to the house, but there are a bunch of people here. Then I considered the beach, but it's going to be busy with the bands, so I'm going to reserve a beachside table at the Lakeside Bar and Grill. I was thinking around eight. If you'd prefer another time just call to let me know. Jenna and Dennis are joining us; he should be here by six, so whenever works for you is fine." I paused and took a breath. "Oh, and just so you know, Kyle and I are together. Yes, we're very happy, and no, I don't want to talk about it."

I hung up and looked back out to the lawn. I stood a little taller as I committed to stop being so weird about everything. If Kyle and I hadn't been such good friends for such a long time, I was sure I wouldn't be going through the ridiculous emotions I was dealing with now. I almost felt like I had the time my dad caught me in the closet kissing a kid in my class who was over for a playdate when we were six.

Geez. I really did need to get a grip.

I was about to head out when my phone rang. It was Roy.

"Eight is fine. We'll be off duty by then, which is just as well because we won't have to listen to our scanners while we eat."

"Did they send someone from the main office to help you out with all the tourists in town this weekend?"

"They sent two someones, so unless something really huge happens we should be able to take the whole night off."

"That's good. You work way too many hours. Listen, before you come over, I wanted to ask about Sam Wilson. I understand Kate spoke to him about Judge Harper's murder."

"Yeah. Someone called in an anonymous tip that Sam had been going around town threatening the judge. Kate spoke to both Sam and his mother and didn't think he was a serious suspect. Why do you ask?"

"I got a tip as well and spoke to Sam's mother today. I do consider Sam a strong suspect, but to be fair I haven't spoken to him directly. He might have said something to Kate that I don't know about that could eliminate him."

"Kate's a bright woman. I trust her instincts. I think you will too when you meet her."

"I'm looking forward to it. I'll see you at eight."

I hung up the phone and headed outdoors to join the others. I was determined that no matter what anyone said I wasn't going to be shy or embarrassed. I was an adult with an adequate, although somewhat limited, romantic history. Kyle and I weren't doing anything strange; I had no reason to act like a shy virgin on her first date.

Just as Jenna had indicated, Kate was adorable. She was about my age and my height, with long blonde hair she wore up but I imagined would be striking when it was down. When I first saw her, an image of a fragile doll came to mind, but it didn't take long for me to see that she was strong, intelligent, and opinionated. And unless I was reading things wrong, Roy was totally smitten.

"How long have you been a cop?" Dennis asked Kate.

"Seven years. I went to the academy after college. I would

have gone right out of high school, but I'd made a deal with my mother that I would go to college before committing to law enforcement and she'd promise not to hound me about it the rest of my life."

"She didn't want you to be a cop?" I asked.

Kate shook her head. "She absolutely didn't. My dad was a cop. He died in the line of duty, trying to protect civilians who shouldn't have been anywhere near the crime scene in the first place."

I glanced at Kyle. He raised his eyebrows but didn't say anything.

"Your mom hoped that if you went to college you'd change your mind," I concluded.

Kate looked me in the eye, paused, and then answered, "Correct. Roy told me you're a teacher. Is that what you've always wanted to do?"

I thought about it. "Yes, I guess in a way I have. It's not like I sat around in high school and thought about taking over the reins from my teachers when I graduated college, but I've always been athletic and I love all sorts of sports, so going into coaching and teaching physical education was a logical move."

"And you're retired?" Kate looked at Kyle curiously.

"Not really. I used to be a full-time software developer, but when I came into some money I switched to freelancing. I help out where I can, but I don't usually charge for it."

"I think I'd continue to be a cop even if I inherited a hundred million dollars," Kate said. "I love what I do. It's important. I feel like it matters."

"Dennis is the new fire chief in Serenity," Roy offered.

"I heard the old fire chief killed a guy."

Kate was great, but one thing was for certain: she needed to work on her social skills.

"It's a complicated story," I answered. "How are you liking our little town?"

Kate shrugged. "It's okay. The people seem friendly enough, but there's a certain lack of culture and sophistication that's found in larger cities."

"I suppose that might be true, but, in general, there's a lot less crime, not to mention noise and pollution."

"I suppose." Kate looked at Roy. "Now that we've finished our meal and the pleasantries are out of the way, do you want to tell me what we're really doing here?"

Roy looked completely shocked by her question. In fact, his mouth hung open for several seconds before he thought to close it. It was obvious to me that Kate was no dummy; she'd probably heard Roy had friends who helped him solve his toughest cases long before this.

"We occasionally help Roy work on some of his cases," I explained. "I don't think he wanted to dump us on you before you had a chance to meet us."

"I've heard about your little group, and I want to go on record that I don't approve. Civilians have no place in an active investigation."

"You've been a cop for seven years. How many murders have you personally been responsible for solving?" Jenna asked gently.

"I solved one and helped in another two investigations."

"Tj has seven murders under her belt and she's solved them all. Kyle isn't just a retired software developer, but a computer genius who can out-research and out-hack anyone you can put up against him, and my husband has been saving dozens of lives a year for the past decade."

"And you?" Kate looked at Jenna. "What do you bring to the mix?"

"I make a mean cheesecake."

I couldn't help but snicker. Kyle kicked me under the table. I guess it was rude to laugh at the fact that Jenna had just torn Kate a new one.

"I don't care what sort of talents each of you have. You haven't been trained and therefore are a liability. My father's gone because some wannabe superhero type thought he could fight crime better than local law enforcement. If you want to be a cop, go to the academy and get the training like I did. If not, stay the hell out of the way." Kate stood up. She looked at Roy. "I'm leaving. I'll find my own way back. I like you and have enjoyed working with you, but know this: if your friends don't stay out of this case, I'll report you and them to the sheriff. Do we understand each other?"

Roy just nodded. He looked like he was going to cry. Poor guy; I think he'd really felt Kate would fit right in with our little family.

"I'm sorry," Jenna said to Roy. "I shouldn't have said all that."

"No. It's okay. It seems obvious Kate has strong feelings about this that aren't likely to change. I guess it's best to know sooner rather than later."

We all sat quietly for what seemed like forever.

"What now?" I asked Roy. "Do you want us to back off?"

He didn't answer right away. Then he sighed and said, "I'm officially telling you to back off and let the people trained and paid to do the job do it. If you choose to ignore my request there isn't a lot I can do about it." Roy looked at Kyle. "Have you ever thought of getting a private investigator's license? It might make consulting with you a little easier to swallow for by-the-book types."

"I hadn't considered it, but I'll take it under advisement."

Roy stood up. "I should go see if I can do some damage control. I'm sorry about the way things went down. I could see how she felt about following the rules. I just had no idea she would be quite so adamant."

"She has a good reason for feeling the way she does," I murmured. "Officially, we're off the case. Unofficially, we'll tread lightly."

"Thanks, guys."

I felt as bad as Roy as he walked away. He was really taking the situation hard.

"Thank you for dinner, but Dennis and I will get going as well." Jenna yawned after Roy left. "I need to get up early to open the restaurant. I think we're going to be slammed."

I smiled at my best friend. She really did look exhausted. "Thanks again for taking the girls the last few days. It really helped."

Jenna hugged me. "Any time. I hope your visit with your dad goes well tomorrow."

"Yeah, me too."

Jenna stood up and then paused. "You might want to prepare the girls for what they're going to see. Your dad looks pretty bad. I'd hate to have the fact that his face is a total mess scare them."

"Thanks. That's good advice. I'll talk to them in the morning."

After Dennis and Jenna left, Kyle and I took a walk on the beach. The area near where the bands were playing was packed, so we headed in the opposite direction. It was a beautiful night, the moon bright in the sky. I missed the warmth of the nights on Gull Island, but I was more than glad to be home.

"How did Blackbeard and Garrett's sister get along?" I asked about the colorful parrot who had provided so much entertainment when we were staying at the Turtle Cove Resort.

Kyle grinned, his eyes crinkling in the corners. "Blackbeard loved her. When she walked into the house for the first time he flew right over to her, landed on her shoulder, and said 'pretty lady, pretty lady.' I think the bird is in love."

"Is she? Pretty, I mean?"

"She is. She's also very nice and extremely intelligent. I think the fact that she's willing to take over the resort is going to work out best for everyone."

I smiled. I'd grown fond of the people on Gull Island. I was really going to miss them. "What sort of work does she do? She must have had to quit her job rather abruptly to take over at the resort with so little notice."

"She's a writer. From what I understand she used to be a newspaper reporter, but apparently she decided to give it up and work on a novel. To be honest, I was in a hurry to get home to you, so we barely spoke. I don't have all the details, but my sense is that she is going to fit right in with the gang on Gull Island."

My hand tightened in Kyle's. "Seeing to the renovations at Turtle Cove is going to be a big job. Did you get the sense she'd be up for it?"

Kyle nodded. "Garrett's sister is at least twenty years younger than he is. She seemed both willing and able to take on whatever tasks needed attending to."

I let out a sigh of relief. "That's good. I felt bad about deserting Garrett."

"He totally understood."

I walked closer to the water and slipped off my shoes, then wandered into the chilly water to the point where it covered my feet. Now that everyone had gone home and the conversation had paused, I found the fluttering in my stomach had returned. What was it with all the nerves? I decided to fill the silence with a subject that didn't make me want to jump out of my skin. "What do you think we should do in terms of the investigation into Judge Harper's death?"

Kyle joined me where I stood and turned me in his arms so we were facing each other. He looked deeply into my eyes, then he used one of his index fingers to smooth a stray lock of hair from my cheek. I felt my legs shake as he spoke. "What I think, pretty lady, is that we should take a break from death and mayhem and wait to talk about the investigation tomorrow."

I leaned forward, my lips less than an inch from his. "Yeah?"

"Yeah," he whispered before he closed the distance and once again made the world fade away.

CHAPTER 11

Sunday, July 2

The following morning, I sat Ashley and Gracie down to talk to them about what they would face at the hospital. Although Dad was doing better, he still had a long road ahead of him and the girls needed to understand that not only did he look different, he was weak and fragile and they'd need to be careful when interacting with him.

"I need to discuss a few things with you before we go see Papa," I said at breakfast.

"What kind of things?" Ashley asked as she buttered a piece of toast.

"You know he was injured in an accident. I'm afraid he has a lot of cuts, bruises, and broken bones that need to heal."

"We need to be careful not to bump him or do anything to hurt him," Ashley supplied.

"Exactly. I know you'll want to hug him, but it might be best if you wait for that until he has a chance to heal."

Neither sister replied.

I passed the raspberry jelly to Ashley before I continued. "I also want you to be prepared for the way he looks."

"How does he look?" Gracie asked. "Does he look like a monster?"

I hesitated, searching for the words that would prepare them but not scare them. "I wouldn't exactly say that, but he does look different. Remember when that kid in your class fell off his bike and had a puffy purple eye?"

"Yeah." Gracie glanced at me with a look of disgust. "It was gross."

"Well, Papa has a puffy purple eye that looks a little gross too, but we may not want to mention it to him."

Gracie scrunched up her nose.

"Can we bring him a present?" Ashley asked after finishing off her glass of milk.

"I think that's a wonderful idea. What do you have in mind?"

"We could make him a card," Gracie suggested. "Maybe something with bears on it. Papa really likes bears. He told me once that they were his favorite animal."

I smiled at Gracie. "I'm sure he would love that."

"I was thinking more like a video game," Ashley countered. "The handheld kind that he won't have to hook up to a television. I'm not sure the hospital would let him do that."

"I don't think Papa is quite up to holding a video game just yet, but maybe we can bring him some flowers for his room."

"And pants," Gracie added. "They never give you pants when you're in the hospital."

Gracie had a point. Dad had a cast on one leg, but perhaps I could find an old pair of pajama bottoms and cut off one leg. It wouldn't hurt to bring them along with his robe, some magazines, and the pillow from his bed.

I glanced at Gracie, who was frowning. She appeared to be

deep in thought, as if she was working through a problem. "Something on your mind?"

"I was thinking about Papa and his accident. I'm glad Papa didn't die when he crashed like Mom did. I would miss him so much."

"Me too, sweetie." I hugged Gracie as a tear slid down her cheek. The girls really hadn't had much of an opportunity to process everything. From the moment I heard about the accident, everything had happened so fast that I hadn't considered how close this might hit home, considering it had only been three years since a car accident had taken the life of our mother.

"Are you sure he's going to be okay?"

"I'm sure," I assured Gracie. "But if it would make you feel better you can ask Uncle Hunter yourself if we see him at the hospital."

"Does Uncle Hunter know you've been kissing Uncle Kyle?" Ashley asked with a mischievous grin on her face.

"No. Not yet. But I'll tell him." Leave it to Ashley to bring up a delicate subject.

"Do you think he's going to be mad?" Ashley prodded.

I really hoped not. "No, I don't think so. You know Dr. Hunter and I talked things over and decided to just be friends."

"Like you and Uncle Kyle were just friends?" Ashley asked with a gleam in her eye.

I should have known this would come up again; I was just sorry it was now. "Uncle Kyle and I are still very good friends, but now we're also dating."

"I haven't seen you go on a date," Ashley pointed out. "All I've seen you do is kiss."

Out of the mouths of babes...

"Look, I want to discuss this with you. I really do. But not now. I need to go upstairs and get ready to go to the hospital. I'll try to answer your questions later. But Ash, if we do see Dr. Hunter, please don't mention Uncle Kyle until I have a chance to talk to him about things."

"So you *do* think he'll be mad," Ashley pushed, I was certain in an attempt to make me squirm.

"I don't know. Now finish your breakfast and then run up and brush your teeth."

Ashley's comments about Hunter's response to finding out I was dating—or at least kissing—Kyle made me a lot more nervous than I wanted to be. The fact that Dad was doing well enough to be moved out of the ICU should have been cause for celebration, yet I felt a churning in my stomach as we pulled into the hospital parking lot. Maybe I should have made a point to discuss things with Hunter prior to bringing chatty Ashley to a place where we were almost certain to run into him. Of course, it was the Sunday of a holiday weekend. Maybe he had the day off.

I took Ashley and Gracie's hands in mine and headed toward the information desk as soon as we entered the building. I didn't know which room Dad had been moved to.

"Hi," I greeted the middle-aged woman with red hair who sat behind the counter. "I'm here to visit my dad, Mike Jensen. He's been moved to a new room since I was here last."

The receptionist accessed her computer. "Your father is in room 212. Just go up the elevator to the second floor and take a right. There's a note here to page Dr. Hanson when Tj Jensen arrives. I'll have him meet you in the room."

I glanced at Ashley and gave her a meaningful look. She

responded with what could only be described as an evil grin. I momentarily considered taking the girls and leaving, but I knew how excited Gracie was to see my dad, so I took a deep breath and headed to the elevator.

Hunter was waiting at the nurse's station when we arrived.

"Uncle Hunter," both girls screeched as they ran up and hugged him.

"It looks like you've each grown a foot since I've seen you," Hunter said.

"Ashley got taller, but I stayed the same," Gracie said mournfully.

"Can we see Papa now?" Ashley asked.

Hunter glanced at Ashley and nodded. "You can, but we need to talk about a few things before you go in."

"Tj told us," Gracie said. "We can't hug him or jump on the bed."

"That's good. Your papa is doing much better, but he's still hooked up to an IV as well as a heart monitor. Don't let that scare you, though. It's just to make sure he gets better extra fast so he can go home as soon as possible."

"We'll be careful," Gracie promised.

Hunter took each girl by the hand and led them to the room with me following behind. Hunter and I might not have been able to make a go of things in a romantic way, but he still felt like a part of the family, and I really hoped that wouldn't change. I remembered how jealous I was when Hunter started dating other women, and they hadn't even been anyone I knew. Ashley might be right that Hunter wouldn't be thrilled to find out I was now kissing a man I'd assured him time and time again was like a brother to me and nothing more.

I hadn't lied to Hunter when I insisted Kyle and I were just friends, although I might have been lying to myself. Kyle had been like a brother to me almost from the minute I met him, and any other thoughts I might have had were quickly suppressed. But when I finally allowed myself to look at Kyle in a different way, I'd realized the feelings I'd had for him weren't really new; instead, they were emotions I'd been holding at bay for a long time. I suspected Hunter was going to realize that as well, and the last thing I wanted was to hurt a man who still meant so much to me.

"Look who I brought to see you," Hunter said as he entered the room with my sisters.

Dad grinned, his face lighting up in spite of his injuries. "Ashley, Gracie. I'm so happy to see you."

Dad's voice sounded strong and steady, which brought a lightness to my heart.

"We missed you, Papa," Gracie said as she took tiny careful steps toward the bed.

"Come on over here where I can get a good look at you."

Gracie glanced at Hunter. When he nodded, both girls went closer to the bed. They stopped when they were inches from the mattress, but, as we'd discussed, they didn't touch anything.

"Does your eye hurt?" Ashley asked.

"A little, but not as much as some of my other parts." Dad smiled at the girls. "I really got myself into a mess this time."

"Me and Ashley can take care of you if you want to come home," Gracie offered.

"I'd love nothing more than to come home and have you be my nurses, but Dr. Hunter wants me to hang out with him here for a few more days. How's everything at home?"

"It's fine," Gracie answered.

"Anything new?"

I gave Ashley a look when she opened her mouth. She grinned and then told my dad she'd moved around the furniture in her room.

Gracie launched into a story about her cat, Crissy, and the mischief she'd gotten into, so I gestured to Hunter to join me in the hall.

"What's up?" he asked as soon as we were clear of the room. Luckily, the hallway was deserted.

"I need to tell you something, and I'm not sure how you're going to take it. I could just wait and tell you later, but Ashley knows, and I'm afraid she might tell you before I have a chance to."

"Okay." Hunter looked hesitant. "What is it?"

"It's about Kyle."

"Kyle?"

"You know he went with me to Gull Island, and although I never intended it to happen, our relationship sort of evolved."

"Evolved?"

"We're dating. Well, not really dating," I clarified, remembering Ashley's comment. "But, well…" I hedged. "We're together."

I watched Hunter's face. I could see the news had affected him, but he recovered quickly and smiled.

"I'm happy to hear that. Kyle's a good guy. You deserve that."

"You aren't mad?"

"Why would I be mad? We broke up, remember?"

"I know. And I still think it was the right thing to do, but I got upset and sort of hurt when you started dating right away, even though you had every right to, and the last thing I want to do is hurt you. I'll always love you. I know we agreed to just be friends, but I want to be sure you understand how very important your friendship is to me."

Hunter's forced smile softened. "Our friendship is important to me too. I guess knowing you and Kyle now have the relationship you and I once did stings a little, but I want you to be happy, and I really do think he can make you happy."

I hugged Hunter. "Thank you."

He hugged me back. I sensed a certain intensity in his arms that I totally understood.

"I haven't really had a chance to ask you how you're doing with everything since I've been back."

Hunter shrugged. "I'm okay. I still miss Grandpa and his presence in my life, but I'm starting to get used to him not being around. It just takes time."

"Yeah. It does. Are you still dating the pediatrician?"

"No. Things didn't work out. I decided I needed to take some time for myself before jumping into another relationship."

"Yeah, I get that." I looked at the door behind me. "I should get back."

"I have another patient to check on, so I'll see you later."

I smiled. "Okay, thanks."

Hunter walked down the hall and I returned to the room alone.

"Papa's going to help me paint my room when he gets home," Gracie announced as I walked in.

"He is? What color do you want to paint it?"

"Maybe purple or blue. I'm getting bigger and the Noah's Ark stuff on the walls is sort of babyish."

My poor heart was breaking. My baby was growing up.

"If Gracie's going to paint her room, I want to paint mine too," Ashley said. "Maybe black."

"All black?" I asked.

"No. Maybe some of the walls can be black and some can be white."

"I saw a room like that in one of the magazines a nurse gave me to look at," Dad commented.

I settled onto a chair as the conversation continued. It was an odd one, given the situation, but it did seem to bring a sense of normalcy to what could have been a very tense moment.

Ashley and Gracie wanted to hang out with Kristi and Kari when we left the hospital, so I dropped them off at Jenna's house. Dennis was off for the entire weekend and agreed to keep an eye on them. Frannie had called and left a message while I was visiting my dad, asking what time I wanted to meet her at the library. I called Kyle and he said he was available to join me, so we agreed he'd pick me up at the resort in half an hour.

"How was Mike this morning?" Rosalie asked.

"Much, much better. He's even making plans to help the girls remodel their rooms when he gets home. I'm heading out to the library to meet Frannie, but I'll be back to help with the guest events this afternoon. Ashley and Gracie are over at Jenna's, but I think she plans to bring all four girls by when she gets off." I paused. "Should I check with you before having guests?"

Rosalie looked surprised by my question. "Absolutely not. This is your home. You can invite anyone you'd like anytime you'd like."

"Good. I just wasn't sure how you felt about having kids underfoot all the time."

"I love having kids underfoot. I never met the right man in

time to have children of my own, but I always wished for them. I'm enjoying living in a house with so much energy."

I laughed. "Yeah, we'll see how much you love all that energy after the girls really settle in. It can get pretty hectic at times. It looks like Kyle is here. I'll see you this afternoon."

Kyle was about to get out of the car, but I motioned to him that I was on my way. I grabbed my purse and notebook and headed out the front door. He leaned over for a quick kiss once I slid onto the front seat.

"I think we should go on a date," I said as he pulled onto the resort road.

"I'd love to. Where do you want to go?"

"I don't know. It doesn't matter. I made a comment to Ashley this morning that our relationship had evolved now that you and I were dating, and she pointed out that she'd never seen us go on a date; the only thing that's new is the kissing. I think things will go over better if we tell people we're dating rather than kissing, so we need to go out on a date."

Kyle reached over and took my hand. "I'd love nothing more than to date you. I assume kissing is still on the table?"

"Absolutely." I tightened my hand around Kyle's. I was enjoying this new paradigm between us. "By the way, I told Hunter about us."

"And...?"

"And he says he's happy for us. I could tell he was a little hurt, but I really believe it's as important to him as it is to us to maintain the friendship we all share."

Kyle seemed relieved. "I'm glad he's okay with things. I was a little worried about his reaction to the news. He's been a good friend to me, and I know how important he is to you. The last thing either of us wants is to hurt him."

"I agree. And I really think he'll be fine."

Kyle smiled as he turned onto the highway. "Good. How did the visit with your father go?"

"Really well. Better than I hoped. He seems to be doing a lot better and the girls adapted quickly to his appearance, as well as to the tubes and monitors he's still attached to. They had this whole discussion about redecorating the girls' rooms when he gets out."

"So you're planning to stay at the resort?"

"For now." I turned slightly in the seat. "Rosalie swears she wants us there, and I think it'll be the best thing for everyone at this point."

Kyle clicked on his blinker and turned into the library lot. Frannie's car was already there. We parked on the side and headed to that entrance. Frannie had asked me not to use the front door so no one driving by would think the library was open.

"I have the book the men both looked at out on the table," Frannie said. "I've looked at it until I'm cross-eyed and I can't figure out what interested them. I'm hoping you can provide a new perspective."

"We'll try," I promised.

Frannie tucked a stray hair up under the tight bun she often wore. "I'm not sure figuring it out will even be relevant to Harold's death, but it makes me feel useful to try to provide some insight. I'm still having such a hard time with the whole thing."

"Yeah." I squeezed Frannie's hand in an offer of support. "Me too."

The book was a scrapbook of sorts, containing a collection of letters, photographs, newspaper articles, and maps. I'd seen several other books similar to this one covering different periods of time. This one, as Frannie had mentioned, covered 1968 to 1978. A number of things had happened in that ten-year period, so narrowing down what the judge and Bristow were interested in wouldn't be easy unless there was an additional clue to find.

"You said Bristow looked at books from other time periods before honing in this one?" Kyle asked.

Frannie nodded. "As I said yesterday, I had the feeling he was looking for something specific but wasn't certain where he'd find it."

Kyle turned several pages, pausing to glance at each one. "We know he's a developer, so it would make sense that he was looking for something to do with real estate. Maybe a land transfer or something relating to a deed."

That made sense to all of us. If Judge Harper had come looking to verify whatever it was Bristow was searching for, he must have discovered something relevant to the strip mall he was trying to build.

Frannie and I stood behind Kyle so we could all look at the book at the same time. Frannie had said it seemed as if whatever the men were looking at was in the middle of the book, but because there was no way to know where the middle started and the beginning ended, we decided to start on the first page.

Looking through the book was interesting. There were photos of Serenity that did a lot to demonstrate how much it had changed in forty odd years, as well as newspaper articles announcing births and deaths and awards and honors. And there were blueprints and street maps, as well as maps that showed land owned by the forest service as opposed to private ownership. Every page seemed to hold something that looked both relevant and non-relevant. It was so hard to know what might be important when we didn't know what Bristow had been looking for in the first place.

"I'd think Bristow would be most interested in anything having to do with the land he wants to develop," I pointed out. "Can we isolate that land on these maps?"

Kyle turned back to a map we'd found earlier. "It looks like this is the county road that used to service the whole area." He slid his finger along a narrow line. "Given the location of the lake, I'd say the land he wants to develop is about here."

I narrowed my gaze to focus on the spot Kyle was pointing to.

"Who owned it back then?" I asked.

Kyle turned back to the map that showed individual plots. "If I had to guess, the plot Bristow owns now is this one. The key indicates that in 1969, the date this map was drawn, the land was owned by Zachary Collins."

I looked at Kyle, who had inherited Zachary's entire estate when he passed away. "How did Bristow end up with it? Zachary would never have sold to a developer."

The room fell silent as we all paused to consider the situation. Eventually Frannie spoke. "Zachary could have sold it to someone who sold it to Bristow. We can search the county records for the ownership history now that we have a plot number. Of course, the county offices aren't open today."

"I can probably find the information online, but I sort of doubt that's what we're looking for," Kyle answered. "Based on the fact that Bristow came in here and spent a ton of time looking for something, it must have been something he couldn't easily find by some other means."

"Kyle's right," I stated. "If Bristow wanted to know who owned the land back in the sixties, all he needed to do is go to the county or, as Kyle said, look it up online. Whatever he found was something he wanted the judge to know about. It must be something that would help him in his campaign to build his mall."

"What if he was looking for something damaging about Harper?" Kyle suggested. "Something he could use to blackmail him."

"That actually makes sense," Frannie said. "Harold was definitely leading the charge in opposition to the development. What if Bristow heard something damaging about him but didn't have any proof, so he came into the library to look at these old books? And he found what he was looking for and told Harold that if he wanted to keep his secret he'd have to support his project. Harold might have come here to confirm what Bristow had told him."

"There's only one problem: how would that lead to Judge Harper's death?" I asked. "If Bristow had something damaging on him, he wouldn't need to kill him."

"True," Frannie admitted.

"Frannie's theory could still be correct if Bristow wasn't the one who killed Judge Harper," Kyle pointed out.

The room fell silent as everyone paused to consider the situation. There really did seem to be so many variables at work. It was hard to focus on any one thing.

"Maybe Bristow was looking for something else," Frannie eventually said. "Something having to do with the mall he wants to build, but not the ownership of the land specifically."

"Like what?" I asked.

Frannie paused. "I agree with Kyle that if he was looking for deeds or other questions having to do with land ownership, he would look online or perhaps go to the county. I also agree that if he was looking for something to blackmail Judge Harper with and it worked, he wouldn't need to kill him. I suppose he could have found something he believed would be of use in convincing Judge Harper to change his vote, but in the end Judge Harper stuck to his principles. Or..."

"Or?" I asked when Frannie trailed off.

"Judge Harper had been citing a building code which prohibits certain types of commercial development within the town limits as the main reason behind his objection to the project. I don't think anyone has questioned the fact that such a statute exists, but what if Bristow found out something that no one else seems to know?"

I waited for Frannie to finish her thought. A look of understanding crossed Kyle's face, but I still wasn't sure where she was going with this.

"I don't know this for a fact, and it may not even be true, but some prior town council could have already changed the code or at least opened the door to changing it, and no one remembers. The statute that Judge Harper has been quoting was part of the initial town charter. It's been more than seventy years since it was written, and Bristow can't be the first person to want to build a multi-level commercial property."

I knew there was one other commercial property in town which had six units. I also knew there was a lot of controversy at the time it was built, but it was a modest professional building and not a retail outlet so it managed to squeak through the permit process. Bristow wanted to build a strip mall with a large box store as an anchor and at least ten smaller retail outlets.

"If Bristow found a precedent set by a previous town council, that could sway the vote," Kyle admitted. "It's pretty much fifty-fifty at this point anyway, so it wouldn't take much."

"But there aren't any large commercial centers in town," I argued.

"True. But what if one was approved but never built for another reason, such as funding?" Kyle asked. He looked at Frannie. "Do you remember seeing minutes or anything to do with town council meetings in the book?"

Frannie shook her head. "Not specifically, but I wasn't looking for them at the time. I suppose there could very well be something in the book relating to a historical town council meeting."

"I know you don't usually check these books out, but do you think Kyle and I could borrow it?" I asked Frannie after considering the situation for a few minutes. "Just for a couple of days. We really need to get going right now, but we can look through it later and maybe find a document having to do with building codes. Even if we don't, maybe something will come up in the investigation that helps the whole thing make more sense. It would be good to have the book for reference."

"I'll keep it locked up in my office," Kyle promised. "It'll be safe."

Frannie paused. She had a frown on her face that made her look older. I could see she was taking Judge Harper's death harder than most—the two had been friends for a very long time. "Under the circumstances, that will be fine. But do let me know if you figure this out. I don't know if Bristow killed Harold, but I have a feeling he's up to something. I'd like to know what it is."

CHAPTER 12

We left the library and went to Kyle's house to drop the book off. We still had a few hours before we needed to get back to the resort, so we decided to order pizza and have our first date. Sure, it was a lunch date and we were working, but I found the need to get a first date of any variety out of the way, and if referring to what we were doing as a date would accomplish that, I was all for it.

"Where do you want to start?" Kyle asked as we nibbled pizza and sipped the microbrew he had on hand.

"I've pretty much narrowed my list down to three suspects, not that there couldn't be others."

"What do you have?"

I set my slice back onto my plate and picked up my notepad. "Striker Bristow, Sam Wilson, and whoever killed Jennifer Reinhold if her husband turns out not to be guilty. In my mind, Striker Bristow is probably our best suspect, but for the purpose of this conversation I'm going to suggest we start with the Jennifer Reinhold case and circle back to Bristow."

Kyle picked up the large envelope that contained the files and other papers from the judge's safe. "I have everything on Reinhold Roy sent me, but it isn't the complete file. What we really need is the original sheriff's file. What we're talking about is trying to prove or disprove that Steven Reinhold killed his wife. If he did, I don't see how Harper's decision to take a second look at the case could have led to his death, but if he didn't, someone else did, and that person, it would seem, would have a vested interest in making sure Steven was never proven innocent."

"Let's look at what we have after we finish eating. If we need more—and I suspect we will—I'll call Roy to see what I can work out. He wants us to keep a low profile, but he also wants Judge Harper's killer found. Roy knew the judge most of his life. Kate might be a by-the-book sort of person, but for Roy it's personal."

"If I remember correctly, Reinhold's wife was found dead in a shallow grave behind her house almost eight years ago. It's possible that if Steven didn't kill her whoever did has long since moved on."

"Do you remember where the couple lived?"

"Just a couple of streets over from Judge Harper," Kyle answered. "In fact, I believe the main reason Clarissa Halloran, the woman who's trying to clear Steven now, went to Harper with her theories in the first place was because they met at some sort of neighborhood block party."

I sat back in order to give Kyle my full attention. "Okay, walk me through what you remember."

"Hang on. Let me get the file so I can refer to it."

I checked the messages on my phone while Kyle went for the file. There was one from Jenna, letting me know she and Dennis were talking about the Fourth of July festivities and asking if we wanted to attend the fireworks together, and another from Gracie, asking if I was coming back to the resort. I answered yes to both.

"Okay. Let's see what we have." Kyle set the folder on the table and opened it after he sat back down. "Steven and Jennifer Reinhold moved into the neighborhood where Judge Harper lived shortly after they were married in 1998. According to statements from the couple's closest neighbors, they had a rocky marriage and loud arguments were commonly overheard coming from their home. Eight years ago, Reinhold made a 911 call, reporting that his wife had been missing for three weeks. The deputy who responded asked why he had waited so long to call, and Reinhold reported that his wife frequently took off for short periods of time after they'd had one of their noisy fights."

"Does it give the deputy's name?" I wondered.

Kyle glanced at the file and then looked up at me. "Clark Leighton."

"Clark retired shortly before you came to Paradise Lake. Last I heard, he's been living in Florida. He was a good guy and a good cop, so if he was the one who investigated the case we can trust his report."

"It's hard to say if he was the official investigator," Kyle responded. "We'll need to try to get the original file."

"Yeah, we will. Go on."

Kyle glanced back down at the file. "After Reinhold reported his wife missing there was an extensive search for her. Not only had she not come home, she hadn't used her credit cards, accessed her bank account, or called any of her friends. Cadaver dogs found her body buried behind the house, and Reinhold, who had a history of spousal abuse, was immediately considered a suspect. The parts of the file sent to me don't outline the details of the investigation; they only show that he was eventually arrested and convicted of killing his wife."

I frowned. "So he'd been in prison for almost eight years,

and all of a sudden his neighbor decided he was innocent and asked Judge Harper to look into it. Why then?"

"I'm not sure. As I remembered, Clarissa Halloran did meet Judge Harper at a block party, which seemed to facilitate her asking him to take a second look, but she must already have believed in Reinhold's innocence. I don't know why she didn't take the initiative to have the case reinvestigated sooner, but she still lives in the same house, so I guess we could ask her."

"I remember Roy saying he was going to talk to her after we discussed this case the first time. I'll need to talk to him and see where he's at with it."

"Judge Harper's notes list a bunch of people, which should give us a starting point if we decide to pursue this," Kyle informed me.

I pushed my plate into the middle of the table. "I'm pretty much done eating. I think I'll call Roy now to see if he spoke to Clarissa, and if he can show us the original file."

"I'll put the leftovers away and head to the computer room. I want to check into a few things relating to Bristow that have come to mind since our conversation with Frannie. Why don't you join me there when you're ready?"

I smiled at Kyle as I got up and headed out to the patio overlooking the lake to make my call. Kyle had a great house in a terrific spot, perched on the shoreline of Heavenly Bay, an isolated cove at the far north end of Paradise Lake accessible by a narrow channel. Kyle had built a dock and a boathouse after he inherited the property, making for a peaceful and romantic place to while away a summer afternoon.

"Hey, Roy, it's Tj," I greeted him when he answered his cell. "Is this a good time? Can you talk?"

"Yeah, I'm at home. What's up?"

"Kyle and I have been chatting about a strategy for our very private and unofficial investigation into Judge Harper's death, and I wanted to ask you if you ever had the chance to pull the original file regarding Jennifer Reinhold's murder."

"Yeah, I downloaded it. It's saved on my home computer. I can forward it to Kyle as long as you promise to be careful and continue to keep a low profile."

"I promise we'll do our best to do both. Did you have a chance to look at the file?"

Roy paused before he answered. "I browsed it. Clark Leighton headed up the investigation. I was out on medical leave with a broken leg at the time, so I wasn't in the loop to the extent that I would have been otherwise. You can read the specifics for yourself, but it seems the prosecution made their case based on several pieces of evidence, all circumstantial."

"Like what?"

"For one thing, there were several domestic disturbance calls made about the Reinholds by neighbors just prior to the wife's disappearance and death. The prosecution argued that the fact that local law enforcement had been dispatched to the house on several occasions set a precedent indicating there was violence in the marriage. Reinhold's defense lawyer argued that all the calls were placed by neighbors reacting to the loud yelling and breaking glass they overheard. At no point had the wife called the sheriff or accused him of domestic violence. Additionally, there weren't any reports of injury to the wife. Reinhold claimed the two were a passionate couple who tended to be loud and throw things when they argued."

"He had a good argument if that was true, but the tendency to throw things could be indicative of a predisposition toward violent outbursts. What else?"

"Bloody sheets were found balled up in the back of Mrs. Reinhold's closet, indicating she was murdered in the house. The investigators could find no evidence of alarm tampering or forced entry, so it was assumed she was killed by someone with access to the house."

I paused to consider this. "If Reinhold didn't kill his wife, whoever did must have changed the bedding. Doesn't it stand to reason he would have noticed that?"

Roy cleared his throat before answering. "He was asked that after the sheets were found. He reminded the investigators that at the time he'd had no idea his wife was dead, so he had no reason to suspect anything. He couldn't specifically remember if he realized there were fresh sheets on the bed, but a maid service came in every week and changed the bedding, so it wasn't unusual for him to come home to clean sheets."

Okay, I could see how it might have happened that way. "What about the lack of forced entry? Other than the Reinholds, who had access to the house?"

"The maid service had a key and the alarm code, as did Jennifer Reinhold's sister and a couple of her friends. Reinhold said the couple had recently done some remodeling and he'd given keys to several people, including the general contractor, the painter, and the man who built the cabinets. He said he got all the keys back but didn't change any of the locks, so it was possible someone could have made a copy."

"And the alarm code?"

"They hadn't changed it. He said that because there were people like his wife's sister and friends who had access to the house, it was too big a hassle to change the locks or alarm code every time they had someone in to work on the house unless they felt they had a reason to."

I glanced out over the lake. I wasn't sure how effective it was to have an alarm if you ended up giving the code to a lot of different people but didn't say as much. "Okay, go on. What other sort of evidence did they find?"

I heard rustling in the background, as if Roy were shuffling papers. "According to the report, Clark also found a pair of gloves with Mrs. Reinhold's blood on them stashed in the bottom of a clothes hamper containing her clothing. Reinhold admitted the gloves were his, but he had no idea how his wife's blood got on them. He said he used them to work in the yard and kept them in his garden shed. Anyone could have stolen them. And investigators found some muddy clothes discarded in a plastic bag in the garage. The prosecution insisted Reinhold had worn them when he dug his wife's grave. He admitted they belonged to him but denied digging the grave or wearing them to do it. He insisted that if he'd been the one to dig the grave and had gotten his clothes muddy in the process, he would simply have washed the clothes. He certainly wouldn't have stored the clothes in his own garage, where anyone could have found them."

"He had a point. It would be illogical not to wash the clothes. Maybe he was set up."

"He maintained throughout the trial that's what happened, but the fact that he waited three weeks to say his wife was missing is what seemed to sway at least some of the jurors."

"Did Clark ever find the murder weapon?"

"No," Roy answered. "It was determined that Mrs. Reinhold was stabbed to death, but the weapon used was never found."

"You mentioned you were going to speak to Clarissa Halloran. Did you ever have the opportunity to do it?"

"No. She didn't answer my call when I first tried, and then I got busy and never followed up. With all the tourists in town, we've had a rash of accidents, drunk and disorderly complaints, and petty theft calls. And I didn't want to mention the file to Kate. She'd wonder where I got it."

"Kyle and I will see if we can track Halloran down tomorrow. If you're as busy as you say, Kate shouldn't have time to keep tabs on us. Although, to be honest, it's not like we're doing anything illegal."

"I know. I just don't want to rock the boat if I don't have to. I'll send Kyle the files."

"Do you know if Kate has narrowed in on any suspects we haven't discussed?"

Roy paused before answering. "I'm not sure exactly what Kate's working on. She's been really secretive lately, and that worries me. It's possible she doesn't want to share what she knows with me because she assumes I'll turn around and share it with you, but I sense there's more to her overall approach to the investigation. I'm being cautious where she's concerned."

"Well, thanks for the help. I'll call you if we find anything."

After I hung up, I headed into the house. I found Kyle intently studying something on his computer screen.

"Is that the file Roy just sent?"

"Yeah. It came through a few minutes ago. I'll make copies for each of us."

I sat down at the desk next to Kyle. He handed me the file he'd just printed out. It was thick, with a lot of witness statements and professional testimony. Just familiarizing ourselves with the case was going to be a huge task, and the possible real murderer of Mrs. Reinhold was only one of three suspects on my list.

Kyle turned back toward the computer while I began

browsing the report he had just handed me regarding Jennifer Reinhold's murder. The main thing that stood out right away was the number of neighbors who had been interviewed. Based on a cursory scan of the documents in my hand, no one saw or heard anything on the day, based on forensic evidence, the prosecution had determined Jennifer Reinhold was most likely murdered.

One woman had reported she saw a man, or possibly a woman, standing in the meadow behind the Reinhold home when she got up for a drink in the middle of the night. She couldn't remember exactly which night that had been, hadn't seen the person's face or any distinguishing features, and could only offer dark clothing as a description, but she was certain it would help them close in on the killer.

Living in a place where the climate is mild in the summer did lend itself to a homeless population that tended to camp out in the forest and meadows surrounding town. Chances were the woman had simply seen one of those seasonal campers, though it was possible she really had seen someone burying Mrs. Reinhold's body. I knew if I was going to bury a body I'd do it in the middle of the night. Of course, I'd also take the body far, far away and not leave it in a shallow grave just beyond the wall of my property.

It really did sound like Steven Reinhold had been intentionally framed.

"Let's look further into the Reinhold investigation tomorrow. What do we know about Bristow other than his obvious motive, the strip mall he wants to build? Could there be any other reason Bristow might want Harper dead?"

"Honestly, I think if Bristow ends up being our guy, we'll find that his motive had to do with his project, although unlike the cases Judge Harper was looking into, there isn't a file on Bristow. We don't have any notes from the judge regarding his dealings with Bristow."

"We don't have notes from his safe, but what about paperwork he keeps regarding town business?" I asked. "There might be something in his office at home, but probably what we're interested in would be in his office in town."

Kyle glanced at me. "How do we get a look at his town council files?"

Harriet Kramer had been the mayor's secretary through three administrations. She was one of Helen's best friends and, like Helen, a major player in the local gossip network. Harriet was definitely not a by-the-book person, so I was sure I could get her to let us into the mayor's office. The worry was whether I could get her to keep her mouth closed about it.

Harriet didn't pick up when I called, so I left a message letting her know I needed a favor that would require a certain level of discretion and asked her to call me back as soon as possible. Like Helen, Harriet believed she could keep a juicy piece of news to herself, but, also like Helen, she rarely could.

After I left my message, I turned back to Kyle. "When you first came back to the computer room you said you had a thought you wanted to follow up on."

Kyle nodded. "The concept that the original ban against commercial properties of a certain size and purpose within town limits could have been challenged in the past is an interesting idea. I decided to find out how the current statute is worded. It does appear the ban is still in place, so I did a search of town council records using the ordinance number as my search term and found eight references to the ordinance being challenged between 1990 and now."

"But not prior to that?"

"The town council records have only been digitized back to 1980, and even then the records are spotty until after 1990. I think going back through the book with this specific question in mind is our best bet at this point."

I glanced at my watch. "We don't really have time right now. I suppose we can come back after we're done at the resort for the day."

"I'm up for it if you are."

I smiled. Spending time with Kyle, no matter what we were doing, seemed pretty good to me.

"How do you think our first date is going?" Kyle asked with a grin on his face as I began gathering my things.

"It's going great. Better than great. It's exactly the kind of date I dream about at night," I teased back. "It's been something really special we can tell our grandchildren about."

Kyle's smile faded just a bit. "Do you think about that? Us having grandchildren?"

"God, no. I'm nowhere old enough for grandchildren."

Kyle continued to look at me with a serious expression. "What about children? You're raising the girls, and I know that's like having children, but do you ever think of having any of your own?"

I frowned. "You're trying to turn this into a real first date where all sorts of awkward and sensitive subjects are shared, aren't you?"

Kyle's boyish grin returned. "I'm sorry. I really wasn't trying to do that. And I know exactly what you mean about first dates and awkward situations. I've had plenty."

"I'm not sure that's any better." I raised an eyebrow. "How about we agree to keep future offspring and past dates off the table for the time being?"

Kyle pulled me into his arms. He kissed my neck and then worked his way up to my mouth. "How about we keep it safe and not talk at all?"

I groaned. "As much as I love that idea, we do need to get back to the resort. Rain check?"

"Definitely."

CHAPTER 13

As it had been the previous day, the resort was packed when Kyle and I arrived. Kyle went to find the girls while I headed down to the beach to check on the preparations for today's contest. I was halfway between the house and the beach when I ran into Doc.

"Did you ever have a chance to talk to Sam Wilson?" Doc asked as I turned to leave.

I shook my head. "I've been pretty busy today. Besides, I'm not sure my tracking him down will go over well with Roy's new partner."

"Don't have to track him down; he's here. I don't suppose the new deputy can object to you running into the man on your own resort and entering into a casual conversation."

I grinned. "No, I don't suppose she could find fault with that. Do you know where he is?"

"Last time we saw him he was over where they're setting up for the bikini competition."

The fact that Sam Wilson was here was a stroke of luck. And that he appeared to be alone was downright miraculous.

"It looks like you wanted to be sure to get a front-row seat," I commented when I sat down next to him in the first row off the stage. The rehearsal didn't begin for another hour, so the bleacher was mostly empty.

"My girlfriend is a contestant. I told her I'd sit up front and take some photos during the rehearsal."

"You should have a wonderful view from here. What's your girlfriend's name? Maybe I can put a bug in the judges' ears." I would never really do that, but I was willing to say it if it would facilitate the rest of our conversation.

"Gwen Jorgen."

I hoped I didn't look as surprised as I felt. "I know Gwen. I didn't know you were dating."

"Our relationship's pretty new. Normally I like to keep my options open, but Gwen is really special."

"I don't know her well, but she seems very nice. I hope she does well."

"Thank you. I appreciate that."

I paused as I searched for a way to continue the conversation. "Didn't she have a cousin or something who recently moved to town?"

Sam nodded. "Yeah. Just two weeks ago. Gwen got her a job at the bar down near the Twenty-Second Street pier. It's not the best job in the world, but the tips are good and Gwen and her cousin are sharing the rent on her apartment."

"It seems like there are all sorts of new people in town. Have you met the new deputy?"

Sam frowned. "Yeah, I met her."

"I take it by your tone you two didn't hit it off."

"That woman had the nerve to accuse me of slitting Judge Harper's brake lines."

"Really?" I tried to appear as shocked as I could manage. "Why on earth would she think that?"

"My mom lives next door to Judge Harper. In fact, my

family has lived in that house for a long time, so I knew the judge when I was growing up. We had an argument not long before he had his accident and the deputy heard about it, so she thought maybe I was mad enough to want to hurt him. I'd never hurt Judge Harper, no matter how mad I was, and I told her that."

I narrowed my gaze as I watched Sam's face. "Do you think she believed you?"

"Not at first. She kept asking the same questions over and over, like I was going to change my answers if she asked enough times. I kept trying to tell her she had the wrong person, but she didn't seem to want to let it go. Finally I remembered my friend from work didn't have a ride to his second job because his car was in the shop and I let him borrow mine. I wasn't planning to go out that night and he picked me up for work the next morning. The lady deputy said lending my car to a friend wasn't much of an alibi. I could just as easily have taken a cab or hitched a ride with someone to get to the community center. I told her she was nuts if she thought I'd take a cab."

I laughed. "I bet she wasn't happy with you calling her nuts."

Sam smiled. "No, I don't suppose she was. It seemed like she was still going to pursue me as a suspect until my mom called to remind me that I'd promised to have dinner with her. Her call reminded me that we'd both watched the same show on television the night of the accident. I specifically remembered we'd talked about it the next morning, before we got the news about the judge's accident. The deputy didn't think that was much of an alibi either, until I reminded her it was a new show, not a rerun. I repeated all sorts of details about the plot that I couldn't have known if I hadn't watched it, so I must have seen it, just as I claimed. She didn't seem happy about it, but she finally backed off."

"Didn't it occur to her that you could have recorded the show and watched it later?"

Sam snickered. "No, I guess not."

As far as I was concerned, Sam had a weak alibi, but I didn't have the sense that he was the person we were looking for. He didn't seem to have any problem talking to me about the events of the night in question or Judge Harper's death in general, and it seemed that if he was guilty of killing a man he'd known most of his life he would have demonstrated at least a bit more emotion. I supposed I could confirm the details of his conversation with his mother about the television show, but I didn't want to waste my time chasing leads that appeared to be nothing but dead ends. While I wasn't ready to take Sam off the list altogether, I decided to move him down to the very bottom and move on to more likely candidates.

Sam and I chatted for a few more minutes before I said I needed to go but would be sure to put in a good word for his girlfriend with the judges.

If Sam wasn't guilty, that left me with two suspects: Striker Bristow and someone associated with Steven Reinhold and the death of his wife.

While I was busy helping with the various events the resort was sponsoring, the girls had somehow talked Kyle into entering the sandcastle-building contest with them. When Kyle had suggested that his team build Cinderella's castle, complete with drawbridge, pumpkin carriage, and abandoned glass slipper out of sand, I'd thought he was crazy. Oh, I was sure that with enough time, the right equipment, and a lot of talent, it could be done, but his team consisted of four little girls with plastic shovels and colorful buckets. I hated to see them tackle anything too hard, but they seemed quite adamant about going with their choice, so I wished them well and settled onto a picnic table under the trees to watch while I reorganized my murder notebook.

Kyle and I would be working that evening on the theory that the book Striker had been reading in the library provided a clue, and we planned to follow up on Jennifer Reinhold's death tomorrow, so I wanted to focus my thoughts. I turned to a new page and jotted down the suspects that were left, along with any notes I had about each.

I began with Striker Bristow. I had a strong feeling he could be our guy. Money was about as strong a motivator as you were likely to find, especially when so much of it was involved. Next to his name I wrote the words *land ownership*. And even if he turned out not to be guilty of killing Judge Harper, I was interested in the circumstances that surrounded a large plot of Collins land being sold to him. Below the words *land ownership* I added *Frannie's book*. I didn't know if Bristow found something to blackmail Judge Harper with or an old forgotten statute that might help his cause, but I did think Frannie's book could very well end up providing an important clue.

I skipped a couple of lines and then entered my next suspect, who, at this point, I could only think of as the person who actually killed Steven Reinhold's wife. Trying to figure out first if Steven was innocent, as his neighbor claimed, and second, who was really guilty if that were the case, wasn't going to be an easy matter. Still, it made sense that the real killer would feel threatened if Judge Harper began to look into the old case. If Steven did turn out to be innocent, I would have to rank this as-yet-unnamed individual my number one suspect. For the time being I listed this suspect as *possible wife killer.*

And then there was Sam Wilson. The guy had always been odd, but there was something about him that made me downright uncomfortable. Killing a man for sleeping with your mother might be a bit extreme, but Sam struck me as an extreme sort of guy. Still, at this point I considered the likelihood that he did it to be a distant third to the other two, but my instincts told me it was too early to eliminate him.

"Tj," I heard Gracie shout.

I looked up to see Kyle and his team standing in front of the best Cinderella sandcastle I'd ever seen. I had to hand it to the man, who had a huge grin on his face; when he said he could do something he almost always came through, no matter how huge the challenge. I was still getting used to us as a couple, but I did realize, as I watched him jumping up and down with the girls as they were awarded a second-place ribbon, that I was a very lucky woman to have such a totally wonderful guy in my life.

Later that evening Kyle and I settled into his computer room with the documents we'd copied from Judge Harper's files as well as the file Roy sent over, the book Frannie had lent us, and the notes we'd made. Since we planned to focus on Jennifer Reinhold's murder the following day and I'd all but eliminated Sam as a suspect, we decided to focus our efforts on Striker Bristow. What we really needed to do, I decided, was speak to the man in person. It was too late to call him this evening, but perhaps I'd follow up tomorrow.

"Let's start with the book," I suggested.

Kyle moved over to a table with conference-style chairs surrounding it and opened it to the first page. "It's hard to know where to start."

"Frannie said the men were looking at the middle third of the book, so let's start one third of the way in," I suggested after taking a seat next to Kyle.

I could feel the warmth from Kyle's shoulder next to mine as we worked side by side. I tried to focus on each page of the book as Kyle carefully turned the pages, but all I could think about was how much I wanted to kiss him. I guess it was always this way at the beginning of a relationship. I could remember being hypersensitive to the presence of other men I dated in the beginning, but somehow my heart knew this was different. I glanced at Kyle's face. He was looking intently at the page he'd just turned to. I wondered if he was as aware of our shoulders touching as I was.

"Look at this." Kyle pointed to the page.

He was looking at a newspaper article dated June 5, 1974.

"What does it say?" I asked.

"Apparently a young attorney working for the district attorney's office mishandled some evidence and it ended up being inadmissible in court. The end result was that a man who'd been on trial for killing someone in a bar fight went free and he killed someone else later."

"Oh, no. That's awful. But what does that have to do with Judge Harper?'

"The young attorney responsible for the man going free was none other than Harold Harper before he was a judge."

I frowned. "You think Bristow somehow found out about the black mark on Judge Harper's otherwise outstanding career and hoped to blackmail him into changing his position on the strip mall in exchange for his silence?"

"Maybe. I suppose young attorneys make mistakes all the time, and I'm not sure if this mistake is one Judge Harper tried to bury, but it seems that at the very least it's worth following up on."

"I agree. Let's try calling Bristow tomorrow and see if he will meet with us."

"If Bristow did kill Judge Harper, he's unlikely to say as much," Kyle pointed out.

"True. But maybe we can pick up a vibe. It seems to me it might be important to find out how the judge responded to Bristow's threat, if a threat was even made. If the judge agreed to change his vote to support Bristow's project in exchange for his silence, he would have no motive to tamper with the car. However, if Judge Harper resisted Bristow's blackmail threat that could have angered Bristow enough to take the next step and make his demands more clearly heard."

Kyle took a photo of the article with his phone so we would have it with us the following day. "Do you want to keep looking?" he asked.

I yawned. "No. I'm exhausted. I really should get home. If the lead with Bristow doesn't work out we can still try to speak to Clarissa Halloran tomorrow as planned. If that doesn't turn up anything we can come back to the book tomorrow evening."

Kyle closed the book, then turned so he was facing me. I felt the heat rise to my face as Kyle cupped my cheeks in his hands and looked deeply into my eyes. My heart began to pound as he opened his mouth just a bit. It seemed like he was going to say something, but then at the last minute he leaned forward and kissed me. I wrapped my arms around his neck and kissed him back.

After a moment, he pulled away. "About that rain check from earlier."

I took a breath and blew it out as I willed my heart to slow. "What about it?"

"I know you said you were tired, but I was thinking now might be a good time to cash it in."

I leaned forward and kissed Kyle softly on the lips. "Now is good."

Kyle took my hand and led me to the sofa. He sat down and then pulled me into his lap. Every bit of fatigue I'd been feeling suddenly faded away as his lips once again met mine.

CHAPTER 14

Monday, July 3

I woke up with a smile on my face. Last night with Kyle had turned out to be very datelike indeed. Not that Kyle wasn't a perfect gentleman; it was, after all, part two of our first date, but first dates led to second dates, which led to tenth dates and the inevitable question of would we or wouldn't we. Honestly, I couldn't remember being quite so nervous about that particular question since the first time back in high school with Hunter.

I had to wonder if Kyle was as nervous as I was.

"What do you think?" I asked Echo, who was lying on the rug next to my bed. "Do I bring the subject up with Kyle and let him know how I'm feeling, or do I just let things go and see what happens?"

Echo barked in response, but I wasn't sure. If I just let things unfold naturally, was I setting myself up for an awkward and uncomfortable situation down the line? Would he be ready to move on to physical intimacy in the complete sense sooner than I was?

I pulled my pillow over my head and let out a long groan. It was too early in the morning to be thinking about this sort of thing. I was sure that if Kyle did make his move he wasn't going to make it today, so maybe I should just put the subject on hold and focus my energy on the murder investigation. The previous evening Kyle and I had decided to dig into Jennifer Reinhold's murder today to see what we could find out after all this time.

I rolled out of bed and headed to the shower. Kyle was picking me up in less than an hour, so I'd need to get going if I wanted to spend a few minutes with the family before I left. I felt bad I wasn't going to be spending time at the resort, but Grandpa seemed to have everything under control, and we all really wanted to figure out who had killed Judge Harper.

"Pancakes?" Grandpa asked when I made my way downstairs and into the kitchen.

"No, thanks. Coffee is fine. Kyle will be here soon. We're going to stop in to see Dad and then do some investigating. Do you have everything here at the resort covered?"

"It's all taken care of."

"Where's Rosalie?"

"She's over at the vet clinic. She does discount shots on Mondays."

"Rosalie has kittens," Gracie informed me.

"Kittens? Where did she get kittens?"

"Someone brought in a stray cat who was in labor. She said there are four. One has stripes. Can we get one?"

"I don't think so. We already have four cats. I think four is plenty."

"We have four cats, but we don't have any *kittens*," Gracie insisted.

I poured some milk into my coffee. "Kittens are really just small cats." I decided to change the subject before Gracie wore me down and we doubled the cat population in the house.

"What are you girls planning to do today?"

"Kristi and I are going to a movie," Ashley informed me.

"That sounds fun. What are you going to see?"

"I'm not sure. Jenna's going to find out what's playing and then we'll decide."

I turned toward my youngest sister. "How about you, Gracie?"

"Kari's grandma is going to watch us until Aunt Jenna gets off work. Did you know Kari's grandma moved into Bookman's big house?"

"Yes, I did know that."

"Are they getting married like Papa and Rosalie?"

"Yes, they are. Now finish your breakfast. I'll call Jenna to let her know I'll drop you both in town to save her the effort of coming out to get you."

Luckily, the girls and I were all ready by the time Kyle arrived. We dropped the girls off at their respective locations and then headed to the hospital to see Dad. He seemed to be doing better with each day that passed. I hoped he'd soon mend to the point where he could come home.

Kyle and I were standing hand in hand waiting for the elevator when Hunter appeared. He gave us a funny look before he quickly recovered and greeted us.

"Here to see your dad?"

I nodded. "How's he doing?"

"Much better. He wants to go home, which I might consider in another day or two, but he's going to need help getting around. Things are so busy at the resort right now, I was going to suggest that you might want to line up a nurse to come to the house, at least for the first week or so."

"I'll talk to Rosalie about it, but that sounds like a good

idea."

"You'll need to set up a bed downstairs for him as well, at least until the cast comes off his leg. If you can get those two things handled, I might be willing to release him as early as Wednesday."

I felt such a sense of relief. "Thank you again for everything you've done for Dad."

Hunter shrugged. "Just doing my job."

He headed down the hall as Kyle and I entered the elevator. Our encounter had been awkward, but it could have been a whole lot worse. I hoped once Hunter got used to seeing Kyle and me together the weirdness would fade and we could all go back to being friends who were comfortable in one another's company.

I waved to the nurse at the station as we passed. She waved back but didn't detain us in any way, so I continued down the hall to Dad's room.

"Tj, Kyle. I'm so glad the two of you stopped by," Dad greeted us. "Now that I'm starting to feel better I'm going stir crazy just lying here."

I crossed the room and kissed him on the cheek. "We ran into Hunter on our way up. He seems to think you can come home later in the week so long as you're okay with us hiring a nurse to help take care of you."

"I don't need a nurse," he grumbled.

"Dad, you can't walk. You need a nurse, at least until you can get around on crutches. I'm going to talk to Rosalie later, but I'm sure she'll agree that temporary help is a must."

Dad made a face, although he didn't respond.

"I suppose I could just tell Hunter to keep you here until you can get around on your own."

"A nurse will be fine," Dad said, giving in. "But only for a few days. Once I get my strength back I'll be able to manage on my own."

"I'll talk to Rosalie about it. I'm sure she'll be glad to have you home. We all will."

Dad adjusted his position in the bed. The poor guy looked so uncomfortable. "I thought Rosalie might be by this morning."

"It's Monday: clinic day," I reminded him.

"Oh, that's right. She reminded me about it before she left last night. I guess I'm becoming forgetful in my old age. What are the two of you up to today?"

I hesitated before I answered. I wanted to talk to Dad about the accident, but I wasn't 100 percent certain if anyone had discussed it with him yet. I didn't want to be the one to bring up the subject of his friend's death if he didn't already know. "We're looking into the accident. Has anyone explained to you exactly what happened?"

Dad frowned and then sighed. "Yeah. Bookman filled me in. I can't believe Harold is gone. The whole thing seems surreal. One minute we were chatting about going fishing and the next he was fighting to control the car."

"Did Bookman mention that the car had been tampered with?"

Dad let out a long breath. "Yeah. He told me it seems someone intentionally caused the accident. I've been thinking about that a lot this morning. I know it seems as if someone murdered Harold, but I'm not sure that's the case."

I crossed the room and sat down on the chair next to Dad's bed. "What do you mean? Of course someone murdered him. The brake lines in his car were cut."

"I understand that, but hear me out," Dad insisted. "I've

spoken to Roy and it seems the brakes had a slow leak. The accident occurred five miles after we left the community center. Unfortunately, the brakes failed at the exact spot where the highway hugs the lakeshore after going up over the big hill that drops sharply toward the lake. When the brakes failed, we were going down the steepest part, where the sharp curve veers to the right. It just so happens there's a significant drop-off in that exact spot. If the brakes had failed almost anywhere else on the road, the accident probably wouldn't have been fatal."

"Maybe the person who cut the brake line was skilled enough to make sure the car failed at that exact spot," I said.

"While that could be possible—although, to be honest, I sort of doubt it—Harold wasn't supposed to be on the west side of the lake that night. If my car hadn't broken down and Harold hadn't offered me a ride, he would have driven through town and then headed out to Lakeshore Estates. That road is completely flat. Harold would most likely have ended up on the beach or in a field. He certainly wouldn't be dead."

"You don't think the person who tampered with the brakes meant to kill him?"

"I think the faulty brakes might have been meant as a warning. I don't have any evidence to back that up, but I do think it should at least be looked at as a possibility. I told Roy as much when he came by earlier this morning."

I paused. Dad made a good argument. If the intention had been to send a warning to Judge Harper and not kill him, it could open up our suspect list. We'd only been looking at people we felt might be motivated to kill the judge. If we also looked at people whose motive might be to send a message, I was certain we'd find new suspects.

"Suppose the reason someone tampered with the judge's

car *was* to send him a warning of some sort and not to kill him. Can you think of someone who might have wanted to send Judge Harper that warning?" I asked.

Dad shook his head. "No. I've been thinking about it and thinking about it and I have no idea."

"Did anything else happen that night?" I wondered. "You'd just left a town council meeting. Did anything that was discussed stand out as being particularly controversial or important? Was Judge Harper worried about something? Had he argued with anyone? Was someone hanging around after the meeting?"

Dad paused and considered my questions. He had a thoughtful expression on his face. "I can't think of anything, but my memories of that night are still fuzzy. I keep hoping that if I think about it long enough something will come to me. You might ask the other council members about the meeting. Until my memory comes back completely they'd be better equipped to fill you in on the details."

"That's a good idea." I smiled at Dad and put my hand over his.

"Did you ever find out why your truck wouldn't start?" Kyle asked.

"The battery was dead. I'm not sure why. The truck seemed to be running fine earlier in the day. I guess there could have been a drain on the system I wasn't aware of. Roy had the truck towed over to the repair shop. He was going to talk to the mechanic to see if he can find out exactly what the problem was."

"Did you meet Roy's new partner?" I asked.

"No, he came alone, but he did mention that someone had been permanently assigned to the town. Roy could certainly use the help. He's been running things on his own for over a year."

Roy definitely needed the help; I just hoped this specific help didn't end up being more of a hindrance.

When Kyle and I left the hospital, I decided to call Roy to ask about his visit with my dad. If Dad was right and the person who'd tampered with Judge Harper's car had simply done so to warn him, perhaps even someone with a minor grievance, like a disgruntled town employee, could be to blame.

"Hey, Roy, it's Tj."

"Hang on."

I waited while he changed location. I could hear footsteps and then a door open and close. After a minute Roy got back on the line. "Sorry about that. Kate is using the computer in the other room, so I came into the office. What's up?"

"You know you're her superior. You really don't need to be afraid of her."

"I know. I'm not afraid. But we do have to work together, and it's just easier not to ruffle her feathers. What's on your mind?"

"I understand you visited my dad this morning."

"Yes. I was glad to see him doing so much better."

"What do you think of his theory that the person who tampered with Judge Harper's car meant to send him a warning, not to kill him?"

"I think your dad could be right. If the judge had gone straight home rather than offering your dad a ride, the brake failure would most likely have resulted in nothing more than the car running onto the beach or into a field. If that had happened he'd be alive today."

I had to admit the idea that someone had simply been trying to scare Judge Harper rather than kill him made me feel somewhat better, although the end result was the same. "Theoretically we can open the suspect list up to people we don't necessarily think would kill Judge Harper but might want to cause a minor accident to send a warning."

"Theoretically, yes."

"That could include anyone with a petty grievance."

"I'm afraid it does. Kate has been interviewing people who attended the council meeting and coming up with a list of suspects based on the observations of those attending. None of the suspects, in our opinion, had a beef strong enough to cause them to intentionally kill the judge, but to scare him? Maybe."

"So far all I have left on my list are Striker Bristow, the person who killed Steven Reinhold's wife if he didn't do it himself, and Sam Wilson."

Roy paused. "I think Bristow could be a real suspect. The person who killed Reinhold's wife seems like a long shot to me. It couldn't hurt to snoop around a bit, though it'll be hard to find new leads on a crime that old. And Reinhold could be guilty."

"I agree it's a long shot, but we figured it was worth a look. Kyle and I are going to try to speak to Clarissa Halloran today. Do you have any new information since the original trial that we should be looking at?"

"No, not at this point. I haven't had time to look at it."

I glanced at Kyle. "Is there anything else we should know?"

"Like I said, Kate came up with a list and is in the process of interviewing the people on it, but I think we should leave that up to her. Let me know if you find anything when you speak to Ms. Halloran. If it looks like something's there, I'll find a way to bring it up with Kate without telling her where I got the lead."

"I'll call you later either way."

I hung up and turned to Kyle. "It sounds like both Roy and

Kate think my dad might be on to something with the idea that someone only meant to warn Judge Harper, not kill him. If that's the case, we might need to adjust our criteria for the suspect list."

"You still want to talk to Clarissa Halloran?"

"I do, but let's head over to the county office first to see if we can talk Harriet into letting us take a look at Judge Harper's office."

The county offices were nearby, so it only took a few minutes to make the trip. Harriet hadn't returned my call, but she was as big a snoop as they came. I was sure we could use her curiosity as a means of gaining her cooperation. Kyle parked in the lot shared by the post office, sheriff's office, library, and county office.

"Tj, Kyle, so good to have you both back," Harriet said as we walked into the lobby of the county office building. "I understand your father is doing much better."

I smiled at Harriet. "He is. Did you know he was moved out of the ICU?"

"I hadn't heard, but I am so happy to hear that. This community has already suffered such a huge loss. I don't know how we would have dealt with it if we'd lost Mike too."

"How are you doing with everything that's happened?" I asked. This had to be as hard on Harriet as anyone. After all, she had worked closely with Judge Harper for the past year.

Her smile faded. "I've been better. When I learned that the mayor was targeted specifically I almost broke down completely. Who would do such a thing to a man who'd spent his whole life serving this community? It makes no sense."

I felt awful for Harriet, especially when I noticed the bags under her eyes. It looked like she hadn't been sleeping much, and now that I'd taken a closer look it appeared she'd lost weight as well. Harriet probably didn't have anyone to talk to about things now that Helen was spending most of her time up at Bookman's.

I offered an encouraging smile. "Kyle and I have been looking into things, trying to find the answers we feel the community as a whole needs. It turns out this particular investigation seems to have a lot of things going on that, on the surface, don't necessarily appear to be related. We had an idea that the judge's role as mayor might have provided the motive and hoped that you'd allow us to look in his office."

Harriet hesitated for a few seconds. I could see that she was weighing my request before making a decision. She pursed her lips, began to speak, paused again, and let out a long breath before she eventually agreed. I wasn't really worried that she'd come around. We'd known each other long enough for her to realize that Kyle and I really did have everyone's best interests at heart.

"What are you looking for?" Harriet asked after she unlocked the office and ushered us inside. "Maybe I can help you find it."

"I'm not sure," I admitted. "Can you think of anything Judge Harper was working on that could have caused someone to want him out of the way so desperately they'd tamper with his brakes?"

"The mayor was a kind man, a good man. He was such a breath of fresh air after our last mayor, who, as you know, was less than honorable. But despite the fact that he was about as fair a man as you'll find, there were some members of the community who found fault with some of his decisions. Most of the people who stopped by to complain had petty arguments I doubt would escalate to the point where they'd try to harm him. The files on his desk would be the things he was currently working on, so I suppose they'd be a good place to start."

Kyle began looking through the papers while I continued to speak to Harriet. "Can you think of anyone who might have come by to speak to the judge, who might have had business with him outside his role as mayor?"

Harriet considered my question. "There was one man who came by while I was at lunch one day so I didn't catch his name. When I got back I heard them arguing. It wasn't like the mayor to lose his cool, but that day it seemed as if tempers had been ignited on both sides."

"Do you know what they were arguing about?"

"Based on what I overheard, it seemed as if the mayor had sent the man to prison when he was still a judge. The man had recently been paroled and was having a hard time meeting some of the conditions that had been set up before he was released. He wanted the mayor to intervene on his behalf, but it sounded like the mayor either couldn't or wouldn't do it."

"And you never got his name?"

"No. But I got a look at him when he left and I remember him mentioning someone named Smith. Of course, Smith is a common name; I doubt that will help you much."

I supposed that a disgruntled parolee could be angry enough to tamper with Judge Harper's car, although Harriet was correct that the name Smith wasn't going to be a whole lot of help. "Do you remember when this happened?"

"A few days before the accident. The timing seemed suspect to me, so I mentioned it to Roy. He said he'd look into it. I never heard back, but maybe he either cleared the man or was unable to identify him."

"I'll check with him."

I looked around the room, which had changed very little since our previous mayor had been in office. I wondered who would take over now. I supposed the council would have to meet and put someone in place before too long. Judge Harper's death was a shame in more ways than one. Not only had he been a gem of a man, he'd been a gem of a mayor as well.

"I found a file on Bristow's project," Kyle announced. He looked at Harriet. "Is it okay if I make a copy?"

Harriet looked over at Kyle. "Is Mr. Bristow a suspect?"

"At this point."

"I guess I could look the other way while you made a copy, but I'm sure you understand that everything in that file should be treated as confidential."

"Of course."

Kyle started to copy the contents of the papers while I continued to look around. I noticed that the pictures on the wall had changed since the judge had taken office, and there were several awards on one wall as well. I wondered who would inherit the judge's estate. As far as I knew he'd never had children; in all the years I'd known him, he'd never mentioned any. His wife had passed, and given his age, I was certain his parents had as well.

There were photographs on one wall of the judge with other people, including one of him fishing with my dad. I didn't recognize a lot of the subjects in the older photographs, but I did recognize quite a few in the more recent shots. I paused in front of one in particular, of Judge Harper standing next to his wife. Mrs. Harper was standing next to Martha Wilson, who was standing beside a man I assumed was her husband. A young boy who looked to be around ten stood in front of the adults. Based on his features and the people he was with, I imagined the boy must be Sam. Judge Harper had a hand on the boy's shoulder, who was looking over his shoulder at him with an expression of adoration on his face. I guess I could understand why Sam was so upset to learn that his mother had been in an intimate relationship with a man he'd always known as an uncle of sorts.

"I have what I need," Kyle said to me.

"Okay, great." I turned to Harriet. "Thank you so much for your help."

"I hope you'll be able to find the person who did this."

"We're going to try," I promised. "If you think of anything else—anything at all—please call me. You never know when some small thing can make all the difference in figuring out a complicated puzzle like this."

"I'm happy to help in any way I can."

I turned to leave when I noticed the phone on Judge Harper's desk. "Have you listened to his messages?" I asked Harriet.

"Why, no. I have never checked Judge Harper's messages. Even when he was away, he checked them remotely. To be honest, it didn't occur to me. I suppose he would have checked them prior to the council meeting, so any messages he might have would be after that point in time."

I continued to stare at the phone. "I know you're worried about overstepping, but I think we should check them. Just in case."

Harriet looked undecided, but after a few seconds she walked over to the desk and pushed the message button.

The first message was from Sam Wilson. "Hey, Harold. I've thought about things and I realize I may have acted rashly. I want my mom to be happy, and it appears you make her happy, so I'm willing to get past this. Maybe we can do breakfast tomorrow. Call me after your meeting tonight and we'll set up a time."

I glanced at Kyle. Based on the message, it sounded like Sam wasn't our guy.

The next message came several seconds later. "Damn. I must have missed you. We need to talk. Avoiding me isn't going to change a thing. You know what I want. I just need to know if we have a deal. I'll try to track you down at the meeting tonight. This really can't wait."

"Who was that?" I asked Harriet.

"Striker Bristow."

I glanced at Kyle again. I couldn't know for certain at this point, but there was a good possibility Bristow was our man.

"Do you know what deal Bristow was talking about?" I asked Harriet.

Harriet shook her head. "No. I don't have a clue."

"Did Bristow and Mayor Harper meet often?"

Harriet paused. "I'm not sure what you mean by often, but Bristow had been by several times in the weeks prior to the accident. When he first brought the idea of the mall project to the council, pretty much everyone was against it. But Bristow can be a persuasive chap, and over time he managed to persuade about half the council members to support the idea. Even those who continued to oppose it publicly seemed to be coming around to a certain degree. I think if Mayor Harper would have changed his position on the project, it would have been granted the support it needs."

"Do you think the mall project will receive the green light now that Mayor Harper is out of the equation?" Kyle asked.

"Yes," Harriet answered. "Unless, of course, Striker Bristow is actually responsible for Mayor Harper's death."

As we left the mayor's office, we ran into Kate, who was approaching the building from the parking lot.

"Kate," I greeted her, somewhat stiffly.

"Tj, Kyle. What are you doing here?"

I lifted a shoulder. "Just saying hi to Harriet."

Kate stared at us with a look of suspicion. "*Just* saying hi?"

"Absolutely," I assured her with a smile so big it felt like my face would crack. "Harriet and I are old friends and I hadn't had the opportunity to speak to her since returning to Paradise Lake. I was in the area so we took advantage and stopped by." I glanced at Kyle. "We really do need to be going. I enjoyed getting to know you at dinner the other night. We'll have to do it again when we have more time to talk."

Kate narrowed her eyes but didn't respond. If she was trying to intimidate me, it was just as well she found out sooner rather than later that Tj Jensen didn't intimidate easily. I put my arm through Kyle's and waved goodbye as we started back toward the parking lot.

"Were you trying to piss her off?" Kyle asked as we neared his car.

"Piss her off? Whatever do you mean?" I asked innocently. "I couldn't have been nicer if I'd tried. All I did was say I enjoyed meeting her and expressed a desire to get to know her better."

Kyle snorted. "You know you're playing with fire, and that, I'm afraid, never ends well."

"You worry too much. Kate is a strong woman with powerful convictions. She's actually a lot like me. I think we both understand that it's game on if she's seriously going to try to tell me what I can and can't do in my own town."

Kyle wisely didn't comment, so after a moment of silence I called Roy to ask him about the tip Harriet had given him. I doubted the ex-con was our guy, but it was best to leave no stone unturned. He said the man Harriet had overheard arguing with Judge Harper had indeed recently gotten out of prison and would have made a good suspect, but he had a solid alibi that Roy himself had verified. It looked like we could move on from that lead. I was really beginning to think Striker Bristow was our man. Roy said both he and Kate has spoken to Striker and he hadn't said anything that would definitively point to his guilt, but he hadn't said anything that would definitively clear him either. Roy considered him a viable suspect and so did I, but Roy said Bristow was out of town until after the holiday weekend, so our best lead at the moment, at least in regards to following up, seemed to be Clarissa Halloran.

"Let's head toward Lakeshore Estates," I instructed Kyle. "Maybe Clarissa Halloran has information that will help us either confirm or eliminate Jennifer Reinhold's murder as a motive for the judge's death."

Kyle pulled onto the highway and headed east. It was another beautiful day and the town was decorated with accents related to the upcoming holiday. I really did wish we were simply on our way to the beach, or perhaps even a second official date.

"I've been thinking about Harriet's suggestion to talk to the other council members," Kyle said after we had driven for a while. "Being a council member I probably should do that anyway to get up to date before the next meeting. Tomorrow is the holiday, but if we haven't figured this out by Wednesday I'll set up a few meetings to see what I can find out."

"That's a good idea."

Kyle pulled up to the gate and I gave him the code. "I think Clarissa Halloran's home is on the meadow, so you'll probably need to make an immediate right once you go through the security gate."

"Do you think we should have called ahead to set up an appointment?"

"No. I didn't want to give her a chance to refuse to see us. One way or the other, I intend to get the answers we came for."

CHAPTER 15

Clarissa Halloran lived just a couple of blocks from Judge Harper's home. Her house wasn't as close to the lake as Harper's, but it was still very nice, in a gated community where crime would be kept to a minimum. When I knocked on the door, a woman who looked to be in her mid-to-late forties dressed in slacks and a designer blouse answered.

"Can I help you?"

"My name is Tj Jensen and this is my friend Kyle Donovan. Are you Clarissa Halloran?"

"I am. And who might you be?"

"We are, or I guess I should say were, friends of Judge Harper. We were wondering if we could ask you a few questions."

Clarissa twisted a strand of her long red hair around her finger in a nervous gesture. "I don't know anything about Judge Harper's death. I heard he was in an auto accident. It was a tragedy really. I only recently met him, although I've lived here for over ten years."

"We don't want to speak to you about Judge Harper's death," I corrected her. "We'd like to talk about a matter he was looking into for you. We understand you asked him to take a second look at the death of Jennifer Reinhold."

The woman frowned at us. She looked as if she might refuse to answer. "Do you work for the sheriff's office?"

I shook my head. "No. We're...freelance consultants who simply want to find out what happened to our friend. We'd really appreciate it if you could give us a few minutes of your time."

She paused before stepping aside and allowing us in. As were many of the homes in the community, hers looked as if it had been professionally decorated. If I had to guess, the furnishings inside cost as much as many of the houses located in other residential areas surrounding the lake.

"Can I offer you something to drink?" she asked after showing us into the living room, where she motioned for us to have a seat on her sofa.

"No, thank you," I answered.

She sat down on a chair across from us. "What is it you want to know?"

I sat forward and glanced gently at the woman, who still looked uncertain. "After Judge Harper died, the deputy assigned to the case and I went through some of his files and found one that detailed his investigation into the possibility that Steven Reinhold hadn't killed his wife. His notes indicated that he began looking into the matter after meeting you."

Clarissa nodded. "Yes, that's correct."

"Mr. Reinhold has been in prison for almost eight years. My first question is, why did you ask the judge to look into the case after all this time?"

The woman narrowed her gaze. She paused, but then she answered, "Honestly, it all comes down to opportunity."

I raised a brow. "Can you elaborate?"

Clarissa crossed her legs and her arms before answering.

"When I was interviewed after the murder, I told the man in charge of the investigation that it was my belief Steven was innocent. He took my statement, but it was obvious he'd already made up his mind otherwise. When Steven was convicted and sent to prison, I thought about doing something to help the poor guy, but I didn't know where to start, so I pretty much let it go. It wasn't like I had proof of Steven's innocence or anything. It was more like I had a hunch I had no way of proving. Then I met Judge Harper at a party and remembered he was the judge who presided over Steven's trial. We got to talking about the trial and I shared with him some of the thoughts I'd had all along. He seemed interested and invited me to his home for a formal interview. I told him I was happy to share my ideas, so we met. He asked a bunch of questions and took a bunch of notes. He must have thought I'd made good points, because I know that after our talk he interviewed some of the other neighbors who were around back then."

"You said you didn't think Reinhold killed his wife. Do you have a theory as to who did?" I asked.

"Not a clue."

"Then can you tell me why you think he's innocent?"

Halloran sat back in her chair, glancing at both Kyle and me before answering. Based on the contemplative expression on her face, I imagined she was trying to make up her mind about whether to take us into her confidence. Apparently she decided to trust us. "Steven and I used to meet to go jogging a couple times a week. And just in case you're wondering, no, there wasn't anything between us. I jog three or four times a week and I'd run into him on several occasions. Eventually we began to arrange to meet at a specific place at a specific time and we'd jog together."

"And you talked while you jogged?"

"We did. I knew Steven and his wife were having problems. We talked about it many times. He told me he'd contacted an attorney to discuss divorce. I don't know why a man would kill his wife if he had already made plans to leave her."

"Could there have been a financial reason, like a prenup?" Kyle asked.

"They had a prenup, but Steven didn't stand to receive any money from his wife either way. He told me that Jennifer had brought a significant amount of money to the relationship. She was the sole heir to her grandmother's estate, and her inheritance was set up so that only another family member could inherit the money should something happen to her. Steven and Jennifer's prenup stated that if they divorced his settlement would be limited to ten thousand dollars; if she passed away before Steven did, his inheritance would be the same ten thousand dollars. As I said, whether she passed or they divorced, it was all the same to him from a financial standpoint."

"Do you know who inherited her money when she died?" I asked.

Clarissa shrugged. "I'm not sure. All I know is it had to be a family member. I remember him mentioning that Jennifer had a sister, so maybe she got the money. For all I know, the grandmother could have arranged everything before she died and a cousin or someone else related to her inherited the money."

"So the only way for Steven to have access to his wife's money was to stay in the marriage," Kyle clarified.

The woman tilted her head to the side. "Exactly. But Steven told me that although he enjoyed the perks that came from being married to a rich woman, their relationship had deteriorated to the point that it wasn't worth it and he wanted out."

"Did Mrs. Reinhold know her husband planned to file for divorce?" I asked.

"I don't think so. Steven told me he was committed to the divorce, but he was afraid to tell her what he was planning until everything was in place and he was ready to leave Paradise Lake."

"And why is that?" I asked.

"He said he was afraid she was going to go bat-crap crazy—his words. He'd already told me Jennifer had deep emotional problems that caused her to react in a physically violent manner."

"Such as throwing dishes and yelling and screaming," I concluded.

Clarissa nodded. "Exactly. I think they were both passionate individuals who had a tendency toward extreme behavior. Steven wanted out of the relationship. He had a plan to leave his wife and nothing to gain by killing her, so why would he? It did cross my mind that he finally told Jennifer he was divorcing her, she went crazy, and he killed her during the course of an altercation, but he said he was innocent and I believed him. In fact, the deeper into things the trial went and the more evidence the prosecution presented, the more certain I was that Steven was being set up."

I remembered there being a comment in Judge Harper's notes suggesting Reinhold had possibly been set up.

"Walk us through your train of thought," I said.

Clarissa leaned forward and glanced at both Kyle and me. She met our eyes before she began. "First of all, if Steven was guilty, why would he report Jennifer missing at all? I know he waited three weeks, which on the surface seems like a long time, but he explained that his wife had a history of taking off for extended periods. He wasn't worried until the statement came in the mail and he realized she hadn't used her credit card since she'd been gone. Keep in mind no one knew she was missing, so no one had been looking for her. If Steven had killed her, why would he call the sheriff? Why wouldn't he just leave town?"

She had a point.

"The reality is," she continued, "if Steven hadn't called the sheriff and reported Jennifer missing, no one would have started looking for her and her body might not have been found."

"Maybe he figured someone would eventually find the body and it would make him look guilty if he never told anyone she was missing," Kyle suggested. "She was, after all, buried in a shallow grave in the middle of a populated area. Eventually someone would have stumbled onto her."

"That's true. Which leads to my next argument. Why would Steven bury his wife's body in a shallow grave behind his own home? If he'd killed Jennifer, he had three weeks to dispose of the body. He had money and resources available to him. Why wouldn't he at least move the body to another location before he called the sheriff? It makes no sense, and Steven seemed like a smart man."

"And then there was the other evidence that was found," Clarissa added. "Bloody sheets just wadded up and tossed into the closet, gloves with Jennifer's blood on them stashed in the bottom of the clothes hamper, muddy clothes in the garage. After three weeks he hadn't cleaned any of that up? If Steven killed his wife, he had to be the dumbest murderer in the world."

I remembered the sheriff's report had said they hadn't

found any evidence of forced entry and the alarm hadn't been tampered with, so the killer had to have been someone with access to the house. And Reinhold had testified that there were a lot of people with both the key and alarm code, including Jennifer's sister, some of her friends, the maid service, and the contractors who had recently worked on the house.

"I just had a thought," I said. "The Reinholds employed a maid service. I wonder why the maids didn't find the sheets in the closet or the gloves in the hamper."

Halloran shrugged. "I don't know. The service I use doesn't do laundry. Maybe the Reinholds had a similar setup. Like I said earlier, I don't know who killed Jennifer or why, and I don't know when the sheets, gloves, and muddy clothes were left. Maybe whoever set Steven up planted the stuff later, after the maids had already cleaned the room. What I do know is I've felt all along that Steven was innocent."

"You've made good arguments," I acknowledged. "I'm surprised the jury convicted him. Unless they had something else."

"I always felt the public defender Steven was assigned was an idiot who did nothing to counter the case the prosecution presented."

"Reinhold was represented by a public defender?" Kyle interrupted.

"Steve's wife kept her money in an account only she had access to. After she died, he was left with ten thousand dollars and whatever savings he had—not nearly enough to hire a private defense attorney."

Kyle frowned but encouraged Halloran to continue with her story.

"Like I said, the defense attorney was clueless, and the

prosecution did a decent job of creating a case out of what they had. They argued that Steven flew into a fit of rage during one of their infamous fights and stabbed his wife seven times. Then he buried her in the field behind the house and waited. When you coupled that with the physical evidence, the history of domestic disturbance calls, and the fact that there didn't appear to be any other suspects, the jury was swayed."

"What did you say to Judge Harper to get him to take a second look at the case?" Kyle asked. "It doesn't seem as if you provided any new information that would warrant reopening an investigation."

"I asked him if he felt the defense attorney who represented Steven had done an adequate job of offering the jury an alternative to the prosecution's theory, and he admitted he hadn't. I asked him if anyone else had been given serious consideration, or if the prosecution just jumped on the husband-as-killer bandwagon without bothering to consider other suspects. He said I had brought up some good points and he'd look into it."

"Have you spoken or in any way communicated with Steven Reinhold since he's been in prison?" I asked.

"No. Like I said, we weren't that close. We were just jogging partners. It's not like I'm on a mission to set Steven free. I just remembered I found the trial unfair at the time, and when I met Judge Harper by chance I finally had the opportunity to voice my opinion."

I sat forward and rested my elbows against my knees, then looked Halloran in the eye. "I asked this before, but I'm going to ask it again. If Reinhold didn't kill his wife, in your opinion, who would make the best suspect?"

She frowned. "I don't know who did it, but if I was

investigating, I'd look for someone who had access to and familiarity with the house. The killer knew where to stash the bloody sheets and muddy clothes to cast suspicion on Steven and had both a key and the alarm code. I suppose it could have been Jennifer's sister or one of the maids, but my money would be on whoever inherited Jennifer's money. Find that out and I bet you find the killer."

It was clear she'd already thought this through. It was likely Judge Harper had already found out who had inherited the money; all we needed to do was take another look at his file and notes. If the judge's death was the result of this investigation, he must have had the opportunity to speak to the killer or someone close to them.

"What do you think?" I asked Kyle after we returned to the car.

"I think the answer to who killed Jennifer Reinhold is a complicated one that may not be solvable after all these years. It's possible Steven Reinhold is guilty despite the fact that it does seem all the evidence is circumstantial. If he's innocent, why hasn't he sought an appeal?"

"Yeah, that occurred to me as well. Although maybe he had sought an appeal and it was denied. We should look through Harper's notes again, keeping in mind who he spoke to and what sort of a conclusion he was coming to." I glanced at the clock on the dashboard. "I need to get back to the resort for the bikini competition, but let's stop by your place to look at Harper's file on the way. Now that I have this mystery in my mind, I'm going to have a hard time letting it go."

CHAPTER 16

At Kyle's we spread out the individual pages of the Reinhold file over the top of his dining table. Judge Harper had gathered quite a bit of information. He had a copy of the original sheriff's report, the coroner's report, the crime scene unit's report, and the trial transcript, as well as the notes he'd kept during the trial. Since he'd been approached by Clarissa Halloran, he'd also interviewed several of the Reinholds' closest contacts: the victim's sister—who, according to financial records Judge Harper had dug up, *had* inherited Jennifer's money—one of the maids, who still lived in Paradise Lake, the contractor who'd been in charge of the remodel, and Steven Reinhold himself. Reading through everything was going to take more time than we had, so we planned to simply skim the documents and get back to them after the bikini contest.

Kyle picked up a stack of pages and sorted through them. "Let's see if we can whittle the suspect list down a bit if we consider only individuals who both could have killed Jennifer Reinhold and could have tampered with Harper's car. The sister, for example. She had access to the Reinhold house and would have been familiar with where things were stored, as well as the daily routine. She did inherit the money, which may have provided enough motive to kill Mrs. Reinhold. The problem is, according to Harper's notes, she moved out of state shortly after Jennifer Reinhold's death, so it's unlikely she's the one who tampered with Judge Harper's car."

"Unless she had someone do it for her," I pointed out.

"I suppose that's a possibility. But if she was going to hire someone to kill Judge Harper, why use the car as the murder weapon? Why not just shoot him or stab him or put poison in his drink? Tampering with the brakes is too uncertain. There are too many variables to make it an effective method of killing someone."

I picked up one of the files and sorted through the notes and photographs Judge Harper had gathered. It looked like he'd put a lot of time into the case since speaking to Clarissa Halloran, which, to my mind, indicated that he believed Steven Reinhold might very well be innocent. "It says here Judge Harper interviewed Sam Wilson regarding Mrs. Reinhold's death. Do you remember seeing an actual interview?"

Kyle picked up a pile of papers and began to sort through it while I turned my attention to another pile to my right.

"I found something," Kyle said. He pulled out a small stack of notepaper that was secured with a staple on the top right corner. I waited while he began to read. "Well, I'll be."

"What?" I asked.

"At the time of Jennifer Reinhold's death, Sam Wilson was dating her sister—whose name is Kendra, by the way."

"Sam?" I was having a hard time with that one. Sam had always seemed too attached to his mother to have any other intimate relationship, though he'd told me yesterday that his girlfriend was a contestant in the bikini contest. Now, if Judge Harper's notes were correct, eight years ago he'd been sleeping with the sister of his rich beautiful neighbor. Maybe my feelings of pity toward him had been misplaced. "Are you suggesting Sam helped Kendra kill Jennifer?"

Kyle continued to read. "It looks like Harper considered Sam a suspect at one point but later changed his mind. He doesn't say why, but it looks like he dropped the whole thing. He'd known Sam since he was a child, and by then he was involved in an intimate relationship with the guy's mother. Maybe he realized pursuing Sam as a suspect would get too messy."

"Maybe. Still, I wonder if Sam knows anything about what was going on at the time of the murder. I know he's going to be at the bikini contest today. Maybe we can slip a few questions into casual conversation."

"How are you going to slip the subject of his relationship with the sister of a dead woman into casual conversation?"

"I have no idea. Maybe we'll have to ask him outright what he knows about Jennifer Reinhold's death. But I'm curious. Aren't you?"

"Totally."

The annual bikini contest was one of the largest and best-attended events held at Maggie's Hideaway, sponsored by a national tanning company that used it as a means of selecting the spokesmodel for the upcoming year. My dad had portable bleachers and portable toilets brought in for the entire Star-Spangled Spectacular, so a large and boisterous crowd was already gathered as Kyle and I made our way through a traffic jam toward the house and the private parking area for our family and our guests.

"I should have remembered the traffic was going to be a

nightmare and started back earlier," I commented.

"If you want I can drop you off near the bleachers and then come back to park."

"Thanks. That would really help. I'm sure Grandpa and Noah have everything under control, but I should be available if they need me."

"It's no problem at all. After I park I'll make my way back to find you."

"I have my cell. Text me if you can't find me in the crowd."

I leaned over, kissed Kyle, and hopped out of his car. I could jog over to the event faster than he was able to drive. Although maneuvering a vehicle through the crowd was a nightmare, the crowd was upbeat and enthusiastic. I'd forgotten how much I loved the energy associated with the bikini contest. Sure, there were drunks whistling and hollering inappropriate comments at the contestants, who were just beginning to arrive, but there were also supportive boyfriends and families who had come out to cheer on their favorite model between the age of eighteen and twenty-four.

"Have you seen my grandpa?" I asked one of the busboys from the Lakeside Bar and Grill, who had been recruited to take tickets and help with crowd control.

"Last time I saw him he was backstage with Noah. The audio system was giving them fits."

I glanced toward the staging area and the makeshift dressing rooms. "Okay, thanks. Do you know my friend Kyle?"

"Yeah, I know him."

"He went to park, but he'll be here after that. Send him back when you see him. Oh, and save a row of seats for Rosalie, Grandpa and his friends, Jenna, and the girls." I did a quick calculation. "Maybe fifteen seats in all. They don't have to be in the front, but I know they'll want to sit together when everyone gets here."

"I'll rope off two rows in section D."

"That'd be perfect. Thanks."

I jogged around the perimeter of the temporary seating to the makeshift stage and backstage area constructed for the event. It really made for an awesome venue. The bleachers faced the lake, so guests who arrived early could sit and look out over the beauty of the water while they waited for the contest to begin.

"Oh good, you're here," Grandpa greeted me. "Kyle with you?"

"He's parking. I just texted to tell him to hurry. There's a problem with the sound system?"

"There's background noise we can't get rid of," Grandpa explained. "Whenever we turn on the speakers there's a very distinct humming."

"Probably a loose wire. Kyle is a whiz with that sort of thing. I'm sure he'll find the problem and get it fixed in no time. Are all the contestants here?"

"As far as I know. There are a bunch of them in the back getting ready. I recruited Doc to emcee the event. He was more than happy to do it, and he does have a way of keeping folks entertained."

Doc would be perfect to fill in for Dad. He had a booming voice and a jolly disposition that others found appealing.

"Do you know if Jenna and the girls are here?"

"I haven't seen them."

"I saved a group of seats in section D for the family and any friends who show up. I think I'm going to watch from backstage in case something comes up or one of the girls needs help changing. Kyle should be here any moment, so I'm going to go ahead and head backstage. Text me if you need me."

"Will do, darlin'."

There were twenty-five girls entered in the contest, all of whom had won preliminary competitions to get to this point. As far as I was concerned, every girl was gorgeous and any one of them would make an awesome spokesmodel. I knew they took the competition seriously, and more often than not I'd settle on a favorite I hoped would win before the finals. This year, however, I hadn't gotten the chance to get to know any of the contestants, so I was completely neutral about the outcome.

"Can you help me tape my bottoms into place?" a girl with long blonde hair, deep blue eyes, a perfect body, and a golden tan asked.

"Sure," I said and got to work applying two-sided tape to her backside. "I watched part of the rehearsal yesterday. The song you plan to do for the talent portion was really good. I think you have a real shot."

"I hope the judges agree. I could really use the scholarship. How's my side boob?" She turned to show me. "Too much? Should I tape it as well?"

"Maybe, if you're going to be doing anything active. Your swimsuit is beautiful, but it's really teeny tiny."

"Teeny-tiny tops are what get the judges' attention, and like I said, I could really use that scholarship."

The winner of the bikini contest was awarded her choice of a cash prize or a four-year scholarship to any university on the list provided when the girls first signed up. Most of the winners chose the cash even though its value was half that of the scholarship. I was surprised to meet a contestant who was after the education that being a spokesmodel for the tanning company could provide.

"What are you hoping to study?" I asked as I helped her tape her assets into her bathing suit.

"Law. The scholarship won't pay for my entire education, but it'll get me started. To be honest, if I don't win, I probably won't be able to go to college."

"Have you applied for other scholarships or financial aid?"

The girl turned around in a circle in front of the mirror, checking for coverage. "I've been looking, but I'm not sure the financial aid thing will be an option. If I have to borrow money to cover my entire education, I'll be so deep in debt when I graduate that I'll never see the light of day. What I hope is that I can find a way to have my undergrad work paid for, and then maybe borrow money for law school if I have to."

"That makes sense. And you look great. Everything that should be covered is covered."

The girl smiled at me. "Thanks for your help."

"I'm happy to help, and good luck. I really hope you win."

She turned and hugged me. "Thank you. You've been great. By the way, before you go, there was a man in here earlier taking photos. He said he was with one of the models, but everyone was getting changed and he seemed sort of creepy. He's gone now, but maybe you should assign someone to watch the stairs leading up to the backstage area. I'm obviously used to being gawked at, but this guy was unsettling."

"I'll have someone come over. Do you know his name?"

"No, I didn't catch it, but he was wearing sunglasses with blue lenses."

"Okay. I'll let the guard know to be on the lookout."

I stepped away from the girl and called Noah to ask about having someone stationed at the foot of the stairs leading backstage. I told him about the man wearing sunglasses with blue lenses, and he texted back soon after to inform me that he was getting other complaints about the man taking photos and would keep an eye out for him. This contest did tend to attract its share of weirdos, and this certainly wouldn't be the first time we'd had to escort someone off the resort.

Once I confirmed that the models were all set and the guard was in place, I headed out to see if Kyle had the sound system fixed. He was on the stage messing with something behind the electrical panel, so I headed over to say hi to Jenna, who was sitting with Rosalie, Helen, Bookman, and the four girls in the seats I'd reserved.

"Is it going to start soon?" Ashley asked.

"In about twenty minutes, assuming Uncle Kyle can fix the sound system. Did you girls have a nice day?"

"The best," Gracie answered. "Kari's grandma took me and Kari shopping. She bought us new dresses."

I smiled at Helen. "That was nice."

"Mine is blue and Kari's is red. We're going to wear them to the parade tomorrow so we can be patriotic."

"That's a wonderful idea. I can't wait to see them. And you know, you have those new white sandals that should be a perfect match." I turned to Ashley. "How was the movie?"

Ashley shrugged. "Okay."

Typical Ashley to not want to show too much enthusiasm. As a preteen, she seemed to have already mastered the whole angsty teen thing. I dreaded what the future might bring.

"We ran into some kids from school, so we all sat together," Kristi supplied. "We might try to go to another movie later in the week with the same kids, if that's okay with you and Mom."

"Fine by me," I said.

"Yeah, me too, as long as the movie is appropriate for girls your age," Jenna seconded.

"Me and Kari want to go to the new Disney movie," Gracie added.

"The princess one," Kari joined in.

I listened to my sisters' stories of their day until I spotted Sam sitting in the first row of the bleachers. He must have arrived super early again.

"I need to go say hi to someone," I told the others. "Let's all meet back at the house when this is over. We'll barbeque something."

"Aren't you going to sit with us during the contest?" Ashley asked.

"No, I'm going to watch from backstage in case someone needs help. I think Grandpa and Uncle Kyle will be joining you, though, so be sure to save them seats."

Ashley looked as if she was going to argue, but everyone else agreed.

There really wasn't anywhere to sit near Sam, who happened to have a pair of sunglasses with blue lenses tucked in the pocket of his shirt. I couldn't just stand in front of him and ask him about a relationship he'd had eight years before, so I wasn't sure what my game plan was going to be. When I'd spotted him sitting there, my first thought was that it was too good an opportunity to pass up, but after thinking it through, I realized what I needed to do was get him alone. Of course, that wasn't likely to happen when his girlfriend was about to come onstage.

"Hey, Sam," I greeted him casually.

"Hey, Tj. Did you get a chance to put in a good word for Gwen?"

"Absolutely," I lied. "There are a lot of really beautiful women competing, but I'm sure Gwen has as much chance as anyone. I saw the talent portion of yesterday's rehearsal and her dance routine was awesome."

"Gwen is nervous about the dance, but I think she'll do fine. She's been practicing almost nonstop."

I glanced at Sam's camera. "It looks like you came prepared to take a bunch of photos."

Sam nodded. "Photos are sort of my thing. My mom used to say if I was around you could bet there was a photo to prove it."

"So photography is more than just a casual hobby?"

Sam shrugged. "I'm not a professional or anything. I've taken a few classes and I have good equipment and a lot of practice. You could say photography is sort of my obsession. My uncle gave me my first camera when I was ten, and I was amazed at the way a simple photo could freeze time. I think I drove my friends and family crazy taking photos of everyone and everything, but a long time from now I'll have visual images to back up my memoires."

"That's nice, though until digital cameras came onto the market storing all those photos must have been a major undertaking."

Sam chuckled. "You're right about that. I must have thousands of photos. You should see my old room at my mom's. There are so many boxes of photos stacked up you can barely find the bed."

"There were that many when you lived there?"

"Well, no, not quite that many. I've added to my collection since I moved out, so now I use my old room as a storeroom. My apartment is really tiny. I do have a few things there. You should come by my place sometime. I've framed some of my best pieces."

Although I knew a pickup line when I heard it, I agreed, then moved on down the row to the stairs leading backstage. Sam had given me an idea. If he was as obsessive about photography as he indicated and had been in a relationship with Jennifer Reinhold's sister, maybe there were photos that provided clues as to what had been going on at the time of the murder. Digging through thousands of photos wasn't going to be an easy feat. Perhaps he'd catalogued them in some way. It would take effort to assuage my curiosity, but you never knew when someone or something in the background of an otherwise unspectacular photo would provide you with just the clue you needed to solve a case.

CHAPTER 17

During the contest I noticed Sam chatting with a man I didn't know well but I knew Sam had been friends with for a long time. His name was Wade Vance, and he had lived in Serenity for as long as I could remember. I wasn't certain Wade had known Sam back when he was dating Kendra, but after Sam left with Gwen, and Wade was left standing alone, I figured it wouldn't hurt to stop and have a chat with him.

"Did you enjoy the contest?" I asked casually as Wade looked toward the area where food and drinks were being served.

"Yeah. It was great. I know Sam is mad Gwen didn't win, but between you and me she never really had a chance."

"There were some strong contestants this year," I admitted, secretly glad that the girl who wanted the scholarship for law school had come out on top. "Did Sam leave?"

I knew he had, but I figured asking about him was as good a way as any to work my way around to what I really wanted to ask.

"Yeah. He's going to take Gwen out to dinner. She hasn't eaten a thing in a week since she wanted to look her best for the contest."

"Wow. I don't know that I'd give up eating for a week no

matter the reason."

"Tell me about it. I kept thinking the chick was going to keel over while she was onstage, but somehow she made it through. I was going to head over to the food court for a bite myself. Do you want to join me?"

Not in the least, but I did want to continue the conversation, so I agreed to have a beer with the man.

"Seems like you and Sam have known each other a long time," I commented as we walked.

"Since elementary school."

"I wasn't aware you had been friends for that long."

Wade got into the line at the back of the bar. "We haven't. We were friends in grade school and even into junior high, but Sam started hanging around with the rich kids who lived in his neighborhood in high school. We basically went our separate ways. We actually didn't start hanging out again until after he broke up with the freaky rich chick whose sister died several years ago."

"Rich chick?"

"Some chick he met when he still lived with his mom. I didn't know her well, but he brought her to a few parties hosted by friends we still had in common. I tried to tell him the chick was a big ol' ten on the weird and disturbing meter, but he wouldn't listen. Of course, at the time, Sam was as freaky as she was, so maybe he really didn't notice."

"Would you say this was about eight years ago?"

The man frowned. I suppose my question had been pretty specific, although he did eventually answer. "Yeah. That seems about right. Why do you ask?"

I shrugged. "I was just trying to figure out who you were talking about." We moved up several places in the impossibly long line. "You said the girl was freaky. Freaky how, exactly?"

Wade took several steps forward. "I'm not one to gossip, but the chick had this really unnerving way of looking at you. It might have been the fact that she was stoned most of the time, but she had this vacant stare and high-pitched laugh that was downright spooky. Of course, Sam was totally into her and she didn't seem to mind his freaky death photos, so I suppose they were the perfect pair."

"Death photos?"

"Roadkill. Sam carried that camera with him all the time. If he saw a dead animal in the road, he'd stop and take photos of it. We weren't hanging around much by this point, but he'd bring the photos everywhere he went and show them to all his weirdo friends. Two beers," Wade ordered when we finally got to the front of the line.

After we got our beers, we sat down at an empty table. I knew the family would be waiting, but Wade's story was both fascinating and disturbing. I wanted to see where our conversation led.

"Do you know if Sam still participates in this particular hobby?"

Wade shook his head. "Once he stopped hanging around with that crowd he backed off the whole 'death is awesome' thing. He still likes to take photos, but I think now he's more into chicks than dead stuff."

I thought about the fact that he'd been taking photos of the models changing and realized that was equally disturbing, just in a different way. I talked to Wade for a while longer and then made up an excuse and headed to the family BBQ. I wasn't sure that a weird hobby as a teen and young adult necessarily made you a killer, but I decided not to cross him off our list quite yet.

"Seems like everything went well today," Kyle commented after our guests had left and the family had headed inside.

"It did. Thank you for fixing the sound system. I'm not sure what we would have done without you." I laced my fingers through Kyle's as we walked along the beach. It was a warm night, so we were walking barefoot along the water's edge.

"I was happy to help. I'm having a hard time realizing tomorrow is the Fourth. I keep thinking of all the things I need to do, and then remembering the entire day is already going to be pretty full with holiday events."

"It does seem that with everything that's happened recently the past few days have blurred together. And to think I was still on Gull Island at this time last week...That seems like a lifetime ago."

"Although I'm not happy about the reason we came home, I do find I'm happy to be at Paradise Lake for the Fourth."

I leaned my head on Kyle's shoulder and looked out toward the water. It was a beautiful night, and the moon shone off the surface of the lake. "Speaking of the Fourth, were you planning to go to the parade tomorrow? I think the pancake breakfast ended up being canceled, but I did tell the girls we'd go to the parade. I thought about stopping by to ask Martha Wilson if I can take a look at Sam's photos, but that might need to wait until another day."

Kyle put his arm around my shoulder as we continued walking slowly down the beach. "Do you think Sam actually knows anything about Jennifer Reinhold's death?"

"I don't know. Before I talked to Wade I thought it was a possibility, but now that I really know how strange Sam was back then, I can't help but wonder if he wasn't somehow involved."

"I thought we decided Sam didn't kill Judge Harper."

"We have. Mostly. But we don't definitively know that the person who killed Jennifer Reinhold, assuming it wasn't her husband, killed Judge Harper."

"Having an obsession with dead animals doesn't necessarily make you a killer," Kyle pointed out.

"I know, but I'd still like to look into it further. I know Jennifer Reinhold's sister had access to their house. She might have brought Sam along when she visited. But I have no idea how often Kendra visited or whether Sam paid much attention to her relationship with her sister."

"And the others?"

"I definitely want to follow up with Striker Bristow. After hearing the message he left on Judge Harper's phone I can't help but wonder what he wanted and whether or not he tracked him down. In my mind, he's still our number one suspect in Judge Harper's death."

"We still haven't gone through the entire book Frannie lent us," Kyle reminded me.

"I guess that's as good a place as any to get back to work. Tomorrow. It's late now."

We walked in silence for a few moments before Kyle spoke. "Are there any events at the resort you need to help out with tomorrow?"

"No. Everything's happening in town. There's the kiddie carnival and community picnic in the park after the parade, followed by the fireworks display over the lake after dark. We should probably plan to meet up with everyone for dinner and the fireworks, but we'll have four or five hours between the parade and dinner. Jenna told me she's closing the restaurant tomorrow so she can take her girls to the kiddie carnival. She already offered to take Ashley and Gracie along, so I guess I'll let her."

"I think maybe we should take a break and pick this up on Wednesday," Kyle suggested. "I'd hate for you to miss spending the day with your sisters."

I hesitated. Maybe we should take a break from the investigation and enjoy the holiday. After all, how much difference could one day make?

I stopped walking and turned to face Kyle. "You know, you're right. I've let this whole thing get to me more than I should've. I'm sure one day won't make a bit of difference. Tomorrow is a special day that should be spent with family and friends."

Kyle leaned forward and kissed me. "I'll pick you and the girls up for the parade?"

"Yeah. That sounds perfect."

I could tell Kyle wanted to linger, and, to be honest, I found that I wanted him to as well, but we did have a busy day tomorrow, and with all that had been happening, I really should spend some time with my sisters. So I kissed Kyle goodbye and promised to see him the next day.

After Kyle left, I headed into the house. I found Gracie in Ashley's room, which rarely happened these days, since Ashley had become so possessive of her territory.

"Hey, girls," I greeted them. "What's going on?"

"We need to talk," Gracie informed me, a serious expression on her face.

"Okay." I sat down on the side of Ashley's bed. It was not at all like Gracie to be so authoritative. "Let's talk."

"Are you going to marry Uncle Kyle?" Gracie demanded

after crossing her arms across her chest.

I paused. I could sense my answer to this question was going to set the tone for the remainder of the conversation. Ashley didn't seem all that upset. In fact, if the little smile she was trying to suppress was any indication, she was rather enjoying my discomfort. But Gracie was obviously very concerned about the subject, and evading her question wouldn't go over very well.

"I have no immediate plans to marry Uncle Kyle," I answered honestly. "Uncle Kyle and I have been friends for a long time, and you know how very important he is to me—to all of us—but we just started dating. It's much too soon to be discussing marriage."

I noticed Gracie's bravado begin to fade. "Do you love him?"

I nodded. "I do."

"Does he love you?" Gracie's voice was little more than a whisper.

"Yes," I answered honestly. "I think he does."

Gracie paused, but I could see that she had serious thoughts on her mind. I hesitated as the emotions she was feeling played out on her face.

"Is something wrong?" I answered.

Gracie shrugged.

I sat down on the corner of the bed. "You can talk to me," I encouraged.

Gracie looked at me with tears in her eyes. "If you date Uncle Kyle but don't marry him, is he going to stop coming over?"

"No," I assured her. "Of course not. Why would you think that?"

Gracie hesitated and then spoke. "Because you dated Deputy Dylan and then you stopped dating him and he went away, and then you dated Uncle Hunter and then stopped dating him and now we hardly ever see him."

Gracie had a legitimate point. If Kyle and I did continue to date, if we did take things to the next level and it didn't work out, would we lose him altogether? I knew Gracie thought of Kyle almost as a surrogate father. I owed it to her to be sure that, whatever happened, Kyle would never feel he could no longer be part of our lives.

"We love Uncle Kyle," Gracie added before I could answer. "We would miss him if he stopped coming to see us."

"I love Uncle Kyle too, and I would miss him just as much if he wasn't part of our lives." I put my hands on Gracie's crossed legs, which were in front of me as she faced me on the bed. "Please understand that neither of us wants to create a situation where Uncle Kyle stopped spending time with us."

Gracie looked at me with an expression that clearly conveyed her doubt. "You said you loved Uncle Hunter."

"I did. I do."

"But he hasn't come over one time since we've been back. He used to come over all the time."

I paused to consider my answer. I could sense how important it would be. "Uncle Hunter has been busy. We all have. I'm sure he'll visit when things slow down a bit." Actually, I wasn't sure of that at all, but I hoped that was what would happen. "And I bet you'd still see Deputy Dylan if he hadn't moved away. Kyle loves us—all of us—and while I don't know for sure how things will turn out, I know neither of us would want anything to stop him from being part of our lives."

"Just because you don't want something to happen doesn't

mean it won't," Gracie reasoned.

I took a slow breath. "That's true. All I can do is promise you that Uncle Kyle and I love each other and we love you, and there's nothing that could happen that would stop us from loving you girls. You asked me if I was going to marry Kyle and I told you it was too soon to know for sure, but I can see a future where that could happen. Someday, after we have a chance to get used to being a couple."

"Would we still live with you?" Gracie asked. I remembered she'd asked a similar question on Gull Island, but that was when my having a boyfriend was only theoretical.

"Yes. Absolutely. You and me and Ashley are a family. Nothing can change that."

"If you married Uncle Kyle, would he move in here with us?"

Probably not, but I didn't want Gracie to worry about things that may never happen. I glanced at Ashley, who was now sitting quietly with a look of contemplation on her face. I was sort of surprised she wasn't making comments she knew would make the situation worse. Egging her sister on was a very Ashley thing to do.

"How about if we wait and talk about this if Kyle and I make the decision to get married. I do promise that, whatever happens, the three of us will live together until you get older and move out on your own."

"I'm never moving away from you," Gracie insisted.

I hugged her. "As much as I wish that were true, I think your opinion of living with your older sister will change over time. But until it does, I promise I'll always be here for you, and I have a feeling Uncle Kyle will be as well."

Gracie wiped a tear from her cheek. "Okay."

I glanced at Ashley. "Are you okay too?"

She shrugged. "Whatever."

I wasn't sure I'd convinced either Ashley or Gracie that Kyle would be in our lives no matter what. I wasn't even sure I'd convinced myself. But I did realize I had more lives than just my own to consider as Kyle and I moved forward. Maybe slowing things down would be a good idea. Maybe I needed to give the girls time to adjust to all the changes in our lives. At the very least, perhaps I should sit down with Kyle to fill him in so he knew what Gracie, and possibly Ashley, were thinking.

CHAPTER 18

Tuesday, July 4

"Here come the dancing bears," Gracie screeched from atop Kyle's shoulders, where she'd managed to finagle an elevated view of the Fourth of July parade. "I like the one with the ballerina dress the best."

"My favorite is the bear with the honeypot on his head," Kyle said. "I think it's funny the way he stumbles around and acts like he can't see where he's going."

"Personally, I like the mama bear with the wagon full of baby bears wearing nothing but diapers," Jenna informed us. "Makes me think of my own baby bears running around in diapers."

"Mom," Kristi whined.

"Tj says stuff like that all the time and we aren't even her babies," Ashley consoled her friend. "If she's this mushy now, I can't imagine how bad she's going to be when she has her own babies to fuss over."

I couldn't help but glance at Kyle, who simply winked. The middle of a parade surrounded by family wasn't the time to start having thoughts about babies or, even worse, the making of babies, but minds tended to go where they chose and I found myself blushing. Jenna glanced at me with a little smile on her face that let me know she knew exactly what I was thinking.

"Oh, look, here comes the high school band," I quickly changed the subject.

"Can I join the band when I get to high school?" Ashley asked.

"I suppose, if you want to learn to play an instrument."

"Can I get one?"

"Absolutely. I think learning a musical instrument is a wonderful idea. Maybe the flute?"

"I want to play the drums."

It figured she'd want to play the noisiest of all the instruments. I smiled despite the fact I was already getting a headache in anticipation of the hours of practice time she was likely to put in. When I was about Ashley's age I'd wanted to play the drums as well, but somehow my dad had convinced me it would be a better idea to learn to play the piano. He'd made a good argument, but I never did get into the piano and quit after only a few lessons. I didn't want to use my power as an adult to sway Ashley from her interests, so I supposed if she really wanted to play the drums I'd have to buy earplugs for everyone.

While I was enjoying spending the day with my sisters and friends, my mind was still partially on our investigation. When I spotted Martha Wilson across the street chatting with Harriet Kramer, I made my excuses and walked in that direction. Even if I didn't plan to ask her to allow me to take a look at her son's room until another day, it seemed like too good an opportunity to pass up. I could at least make an appointment with her now.

"Martha, Harriet," I greeted. "I'm so happy to have run into you."

"You needed something?" Harriet asked.

"Actually, I wanted to ask Martha if she'd mind if I stopped by tomorrow or the next day. I have a few more questions, if you have the time."

"I'm afraid I'm leaving early in the morning to visit my sister. I'm still having a hard time dealing with Harold's death, and I thought some time away would be good for me. I'm on my way to the hairdresser now, but I'll be home later this afternoon if you'd like to stop by then."

"I would like that very much. Say around three?"

"Three is fine."

After chatting with the women a few more minutes, I jogged back across the street to where Kyle and the others were waiting.

"Was she willing to speak with us?" Kyle asked.

"Yes, but it has to be today. She's leaving early tomorrow morning to visit her sister. I told her we'd be by at three."

Kyle grimaced.

"That's a bad time?"

"I was going to wait to tell you this, but I made an appointment for three."

I shrugged. "That's okay. I can go alone." I turned to Jenna. "As long as Jenna doesn't mind watching the girls for an hour or so."

"I don't mind at all," Jenna confirmed.

Jenna was a wonderful friend who was always willing to help when I needed her. I owed her at least a thousand hours of babysitting in kind, although she'd never once brought it up.

"There'll be a food court over in the park if you want to come and have lunch with us before your meetings," Jenna offered.

"I'm starving. A good old-fashioned chili dog sounds

perfect," I said. "Kyle will need to run me out to the resort to pick up Grandpa's truck, but we should have plenty of time to eat first."

"We really do need to see about getting you a new car," Kyle commented.

I wanted to remind him that I could take care of getting my own car, but instead I just smiled and said I would welcome his help with the task as soon as we could find a day to head down to Reno to visit the car lots. I fully intended to both select and pay for my own car, but it wouldn't kill me to be nice to the man who'd watched the entire parade with an eight-year-old sitting on his shoulders. Gracie was eating up his extra attention, her somber mood of the previous evening completely gone.

"Who are you meeting?" I asked him after we'd arrived at the park and the four girls had gone off to play on the swings while we waited for our food.

"Bristow's administrative assistant. I knew Bristow was out of town until after the holiday, but I used my town council connections to get in touch with his assistant. I figure if Bristow is our man he's not going to tell us anything anyway, but the assistant might be willing to talk for a price. I called him and it turned out he was open to a conversation, especially when I let him know I was willing to pay for information. I was going to tell you about the meeting when I had the chance. I agreed, at his insistence, to go alone."

"That's fine; it turned out just as well. Maybe the assistant will have the information we need to put this mystery to bed."

*   *   *

Martha had made lemonade again, which she served on the patio as soon as I arrived. I felt bad that I had to question the poor woman again; she was taking Judge Harper's death really hard. I could understand that. Not only had she lost a man she'd cared enough about to become intimate with, she'd lost a friend she shared her evenings playing cards and dining with as well.

"How can I help you?" Martha asked when we'd both taken our seats.

"I've come across some interesting files that Judge Harper was looking into when he died."

"Recent files?"

"More like recent notes on older cases. One of the ones he was working on related to a murder that occurred eight years ago in this very neighborhood."

A look of recognition crossed Martha's face. "You must mean Jennifer Reinhold. Such a tragedy. Jennifer's own husband killed her and buried her behind the house. I remember thinking at the time that there could be no bigger betrayal than to be murdered by the man you vowed to love for eternity."

"Yes, it really was a tragedy. The reason I'm here now is because I ran into Sam at the resort yesterday, and he told me about his photography hobby. He mentioned he kept most of his old photos here at your house, and I was hoping you'd let me look at them."

Surprise showed on Martha's face. "Why ever would you want to look at Sam's photos? I thought you believed me when I told you he wouldn't have killed Harold."

"I do believe you," I assured her. "The thing is, reading the judge's file piqued my curiosity. I knew a woman died in this neighborhood, and I knew Sam recorded all sorts of ordinary moments in photographs. I was hoping he might have photographs of the neighborhood at the time of the murder that could contain clues."

Martha took a moment before answering. "Have you asked Sam about looking at his photos?"

"No," I admitted. "We did chat about them yesterday, but it didn't occur to me that his photos could provide new insight and evidence until later. I was going to call to ask his permission, but because you're going away in the morning…"

Martha hesitated again. "I can call him to ask if it would be all right. Do you think that woman's murder had anything to do with what happened to Harold?"

"I don't know," I answered honestly. "It might. I figured there was no harm in following up on an idea."

Martha got up. "Let me just call Sam. If it's all right with him, it's all right with me."

I knew there was a huge risk Sam would say it definitely wasn't okay for me to look through his boxes, but I didn't have a choice. When Mrs. Wilson returned to the patio she informed me that Sam hadn't answered his phone, but she'd thought it over and realized he most likely wouldn't mind if it would help us track down Harold's killer.

She showed me to his room, which was filled from floor to ceiling with boxes, then headed back into another room to answer the phone. I just hoped the call wasn't from Sam, insisting I wasn't to be permitted to look at his photos.

At first it seemed as if there were way too many boxes to make a search for a specific time period possible, but after I opened a few of them and sorted through the photos on the top,

I could see the boxes had been stacked in a loose chronological order. All I needed to do was figure out which area of the room contained boxes from about eight years ago. Because the boxes weren't labeled, I'd need to depend on my recognition of something in one of the photos inside that would indicate a year.

It was both fun and creepy to search through the boxes. Sam really was a talented photographer and he seemed to have captured everything on film. Many of his photos seemed to be of inconsequential items that most people would never think to photograph, which I supposed could be explained by his own use of the term "obsession." There were also quite a few photographs that were disturbing in nature. Not only did I come across the roadkill photos, which were incredibly gross, but there were also other photos of dead subjects such as a dead squirrel, a woman lying in a coffin, and a car accident that I was certain no one had survived. The man seemed to have a fascination with every aspect of life including the good, the bad, and the downright disturbing.

After the fiftieth photo of a dead animal or terrible accident, I was seriously beginning to consider dropping the whole thing when I came across a box that contained photos of some people standing in front of a house I was sure was the one the Reinholds had lived in. There were eight people in one photo. I didn't know most of them, but I did recognize Steven and Jennifer Reinhold from their photos in Judge Harper's file. Could the woman standing next to Jennifer be her sister, Kendra?

The photo was enough to convince me to continue to look through that box. I picked up the next batch of photos and was sorting through them when I heard the doorbell ring. I could hear Martha speaking to someone—a man—but I doubted Sam would ring the bell at his own mother's home, so I continued my search. It wasn't until I was near the bottom of the box that I found a photo that was much more than I'd been looking for.

I placed my hand to my mouth to stifle the scream I could feel building up. I needed to call Roy, and I needed to call him immediately. But not from there. I put the photo in my pocket and returned the box to the place I'd found it. I left the room and moved through the house, approaching the room just inside the patio, where Mrs. Wilson was speaking with the man. I was still pretty sure it wasn't Sam, but I wasn't certain, so I slipped closer until I could more clearly make out their conversation. I let out a slow breath when I realized it was a deliveryman; Mrs. Wilson had invited him for a glass of lemonade. Based on the familiar way they were chatting, I was willing to bet the man had stopped in for a drink on more than one occasion.

"Are you finished, dear?" Mrs. Wilson asked.

"I am, thank you. I need to go meet my family, but I do appreciate the opportunity to enjoy your son's art. Have a nice time visiting your sister."

"I'm looking forward to the trip."

"I'll see you when you get back."

I wasn't sure why I felt nervous when the man followed me through the house, but I did. I supposed it could be the damning piece of evidence I had in my pocket. I made it outside and slipped into Grandpa's truck, sighing in relief when I saw the man drive away. I decided to wait to call Roy until I'd left the gated community and returned to the highway. Once I felt comfortable that I had put enough distance between myself and Martha's house, I'd pull over and call the detective, who would be very interested in the fact that Sam Wilson had a photograph of Jennifer Reinhold's bloody body in the shallow grave before she was covered.

"Roy, it's Tj."

"Tj, I'm glad you called. I was just about to let you know that Kate solved the case."

"She did?"

"Her interviews of the people who attended the town council meeting finally paid off. She found an eyewitness who saw Sam Wilson crawling around under Judge Harper's car that night. It looks like he did intend to send him a warning to back off from seeing his mother. I think he had no idea how it would end up, but I'm sure he'll be found guilty of manslaughter despite his intention. Kate is on her way over to his place to arrest him right now."

"Alone?"

"Yeah. I'm tied up with a four-car pileup I need to get back to. I'll..."

"Roy?" I said.

I looked at my phone. The battery was totally dead. I searched around in the glove box for a charger, but Grandpa didn't have one. I could go back to Mrs. Wilson's and call Roy back. I hated for the news that her son had killed both Jennifer Reinhold and Judge Harper to be broken to her in quite this way, but Mrs. Wilson's house was the closest one I could think of, and Kate had no idea how dangerous Sam really was. I wanted to get her a message before she confronted him, and I didn't want to take the time to drive into town.

I made a quick decision and turned the truck around, heading back toward Mrs. Wilson's. As I was nearing the security gate, I saw a car pass through that looked a lot like Sam's. If he wasn't at his apartment, Kate wasn't in danger, so I thought perhaps I should drive to town and phone Roy from there. I was about to do just that when the voice in my head told me to check things out at the house to be certain I really had seen Sam on his way there. I drove through the gate and continued slowly to the house I'd just left.

If Sam was there, I didn't want him to see me, so I drove past the house and circled around. His car was definitely in front of Mrs. Wilson's house. If Sam was here instead of home, Kate most likely wasn't in imminent danger. I pulled over to check my phone one more time. It was still dead. I was about to pull away and head back into town when I heard what sounded like a gunshot. I didn't stop to think. I opened my car door and ran as fast as I could toward the house. Surely Sam wouldn't kill his own mother.

Once I arrived at the house, I had the presence of mind to look through the open window. Martha Wilson was standing in the living room, crying and begging Sam to stop what he was doing. Sam was standing in the middle of the room holding a gun. It was then I saw Kate kneeling on the floor. Her shoulder was bleeding, but she was conscious. Sam was screaming for his mother to pack a bag, but she seemed frozen in place. It took me a minute to understand what I was seeing. Kate went to Sam's apartment to arrest him. Maybe he'd been leaving to head over to his mother's and she'd followed him. Or maybe she'd decided to come to speak to Martha for some reason before arresting Sam. For the first time since I'd arrived, I noticed the sheriff's department vehicle off to the side of the house.

I took out my phone and shook it. Still dead. The way Sam was screaming, I had no doubt he'd kill Kate if I didn't intervene. Maybe I could make it to her vehicle and use her radio to call for help. I'd have to pass in front of the window to get to the car, so I crouched down as much as I could and began to move. I arrived at the car only to find it locked. Damn.

I heard another shot. I ran back toward the house and looked in the window. Kate's other shoulder was bleeding. Was he planning to kill her slowly? That made no sense. I knew I needed to act, and I needed to do it quickly, but I had no plan.

"Please stop." Martha was crying. "You can't do this. Please, we can work something out."

"Shut up," Sam shouted. "Now go get a bag or I'll put another bullet in our visitor."

Martha turned and walked down the hall. This, I realized, was my chance. I headed around to the side of the house, where I suspected Martha's bedroom was. When she entered, I knocked on the window. She hesitated for just a few seconds and then opened it for me. I climbed in.

"We need to call for help."

"They'll arrest Sammy."

"Yes, they will, but if we don't get help he'll kill the deputy. Is there a phone in this part of the house?"

"No. Just in the kitchen. On the other side of the living room."

"Do you have a cell phone?"

Martha shook her head.

"Come on, Mom. We have to go," Sam called out.

"Go," I instructed Martha. "Try to create a diversion when you get back to the living room."

"A diversion?"

"Pretend to faint or, better yet, have a heart attack."

Martha looked uncertain.

"Just do it. If you don't and Sam kills the deputy it will be partially your fault."

Tears were streaming down Martha's face, but I could see

she would do as I asked. I grabbed a cane that was leaning against the wall and followed Martha back down the hall, staying far enough back that I hoped Sam wouldn't see me. He might have heard me, though, because he glanced in my direction before Martha screamed and grabbed her chest.

As Martha fell to the floor, Sam set the gun to his side and went to help her. I snuck up behind him and hit him as hard as I could with the cane. Luckily, it was hard enough to knock him over. I grabbed the gun before telling Mrs. Wilson to go into the kitchen and dial 911.

Sam recovered quickly from my attack. He jumped up and came after me. I didn't even think, I just pointed the gun and pulled the trigger.

Luckily, I shot him in the leg. I honestly wasn't certain what I would have done if I'd killed him.

"You stupid bitch!" Sam yelled at me. His eyes had the look of a rabid dog.

"Stay down," I demanded in the most authoritative voice I could muster.

Sam ignored me and started to get up, so I pulled the trigger again, this time hitting the wall behind him.

Mrs. Wilson was hysterical by this point. She was wailing and crying as she tried to comfort Sam, who was totally ignoring her.

"Get the deputy's handcuffs," I said to Mrs. Wilson.

Kate was lying on the floor in a pool of blood and I knew she wouldn't be able to help me. I just needed to hang on until help arrived.

"Why?" Mrs. Wilson cried. "What are you going to do?"

"We need to cuff Sam until help arrives."

Mrs. Wilson cried harder, but she didn't make a move to do

as I said. I could tell I was in this alone. Sam started to move and I pointed the gun at his head. "If I need to use another bullet, I'm going to make it count."

Mrs. Wilson fainted and Sam began yelling and cussing, but at least he was staying put. At least for the time being. I glanced at Kate. She was out cold. I hoped she wasn't dead, but I couldn't tell, and I didn't take my eyes off Sam for even one minute to check on her.

"Did you kill Jennifer Reinhold?" I demanded. I really didn't expect Sam to answer, but if I could divert him from the onslaught of cussing even for a minute it might help my migraine that was developing.

"What's it to you?" Sam spat back.

His eyes were filled with rage. I really couldn't tell what he might do next. I was scared out of my mind, but I decided to play it cool. I shrugged, never taking my eyes off Sam or my finger off the trigger. My arm was beginning to shake. I wasn't sure how long I could hold out. Where was Roy? It seemed like he should have been here by now.

Sam must have noticed that my arm was shaking, because once the sirens could be heard in the distance he made one last attempt to lunge at me. I pulled the trigger without taking the time to aim. It hit him in the arm. Mrs. Wilson came to and started yelling, but I maintained my position. By the time Roy came to take over my knees were so wobbly I had to grab onto the sofa to keep from falling to the floor.

Roy cuffed Sam, then ran over to check on Kate.

"How is she?"

"Alive, thanks to you. The ambulance is on the way. What happened?"

"I don't know. I came to Martha's place to look at Sam's

photographs. I thought I might find a clue leading to the truth about Jennifer Reinhold's death."

"Did you?"

I handed Roy the photo from my pocket.

"Sam killed Mrs. Reinhold?"

"It looks that way. At the very least he was an accomplice."

"Do you know how Kate ended up here?"

"No. I was going to tell you about the photo, but my phone died when we were talking. I came back here to use Mrs. Wilson's phone to call you and saw Sam's car. I was about to leave when I heard a gunshot. When I made my way to the house I noticed Kate's car. I guess she decided to come to speak to Mrs. Wilson for some reason. Sam showed up sometime before I arrived the second time. Somehow he must have gotten the upper hand on her. He had her gun and shot her with it. I hope she's okay."

Roy glanced out the window as a pair of ambulances arrived. He took charge of transferring Sam into one while the EMTs loaded Kate into the other. I decided to join Mrs. Wilson on the sofa. She was sitting perfectly still, staring into space. I hoped the shock wasn't too much for her. She was at an age where such an upset like this could really give her a heart attack.

Later that evening I sat on the beach as colorful explosions lit the night sky. The day, which had started out simply lovely with family and friends together, was ending that way as well despite the part in the middle. I relaxed into Kyle's arms as he supported my weight while we sat on the blanket with Ashley, Gracie, Jenna and her girls, Grandpa, Doc, Bookman and Helen, and Rosalie, along with a puppy she'd found on the beach and was keeping an eye on until she could locate the owner. I watched the tender way she calmed the frightened pup and realized it really was a shame she'd missed her shot at having children of her own. She had a wonderful nurturing way about her. But she was going to make a fantastic grandma for Ashley and Gracie, who'd never had one before. And maybe one day, if Kyle and I did marry and have children, she'd make a terrific grandmother for them as well.

"Oh, wow, did you see that?" Gracie stood up. She clapped her hands as she jumped up and down in place. Ashley got up and joined her, and before I knew it, all four girls were jumping and clapping with each new explosion overhead.

"I like the silver streamers," Ashley insisted when Kristi announced that her favorite were the red, white, and blue buttons that exploded into flowers.

Gracie was so wound up she was spinning in circles while she looked up into the dark sky. I knew that years from now she and Ashley would remember these family moments the way I remembered the ones from my childhood.

I could feel Kyle's heart beat against my back as I leaned into him. This was shaping up to be one of my favorite fireworks shows yet. The only thing that could have made it even more perfect would have been Judge Harper kicking off the festivities as the acting mayor always had.

Once I had been interviewed by Roy, I'd gone back to the resort to find Kyle waiting for me. He'd been able to confirm that Bristow had indeed been trying to blackmail Judge Harper using the information he had found about Harper's mistake as a young attorney. Reputation was very important to Bristow, even if it was mostly considered to be a bad one, so he'd just assumed Judge Harper could be swayed to seeing things his way if he could find the right kind of dirt on him. Kyle had called Bookman and several of the other council members and, although Bristow hadn't been the one to tamper with Judge Harper's car, his actions were still seen as unconscionable. The mall, as far as Kyle could tell, was pretty much dead in the water.

Gracie laughed as Kyle jumped up and chased her for putting sand down his shirt. As he picked her up and threatened to toss her into the lake, I had a very vivid memory of doing the same song and dance with my dad. Ashley tried to overpower Kyle to save her sister, and before I knew it, all four girls had tackled him to the ground. I was really missing my dad tonight, although Hunter had assured me he would make a full recovery. He was coming home tomorrow.

As I watched my family share this special event on the beach we called home, I knew without a doubt that, despite the temporary insanity that had sent me running across the country, Paradise Lake was where I was meant to be.

CHAPTER 19

Wednesday, July 5

"He's here, he's here," Gracie shouted, running through the house as soon as she spied Rosalie's car pulling onto the resort road from the second-story window.

"Remember, we need to be gentle," I called as both sisters and the dogs ran for the front door. Luckily, Kyle and Grandpa had both gone with Rosalie to help bring Dad home, so Kyle intercepted the dogs while Grandpa intercepted the girls.

The nurse Rosalie had hired stood off to the side, waiting to get Dad settled after everyone had greeted him. Once the girls had a chance to say their hellos, I wandered over to give him a gentle hug and a kiss on the cheek. "Welcome home. We're so happy you're here."

Dad tried to squeeze my hand, but he was still weak. "Not as happy as I am to be here."

"We have a temporary room all set up for you in the den. The nurse wants to get you settled—check your vitals and all that—so I'm going to take the girls and the dogs down to the beach. We'll talk later."

Dad smiled. "Okay, sweetheart. Thank you for everything."

Kyle joined Ashley, Gracie, Echo, Pumpkin, Trooper, and me as we headed to the picnic area I'd set up. Both girls, along with all the dogs, jumped into the cool, clear water as Kyle and I set about making sandwiches.

"Thanks for going with Rosalie," I said as Kyle smeared mustard on several slices of bread.

"I was more than happy to help. That's what families do. Mike seems to be in good spirits, and I had a chat with Hunter while we waited for the nurse to get him ready to go. He seems to think Mike's going to be just fine."

"How was it? Your chat with Hunter?"

Kyle shrugged. "It was fine. It wasn't even weird. I honestly think he's happy for us. I'm sure there'll be moments of awkwardness from time to time, but Hunter will make his adjustments and we'll be able to get back to normal. How did your meeting with Roy go?"

One of the reasons I hadn't gone with the others to get Dad was because Roy had stopped by to take my statement just as everyone was leaving.

"It went fine. Sam admitted he'd helped Kendra kill her sister eight years ago and frame Steven Reinhold. He said they were after the money, which Kendra had agreed to give him a cut of, but then she stiffed him after he'd helped her. There wasn't much he could do at that point; he couldn't expose her without exposing himself."

"And his mother?"

"Martha went to her sister's as planned. I wouldn't be surprised if she stays there permanently. I think Paradise Lake has lost its appeal for her. After living here for a lifetime, it really is too bad she'll probably take away more bad memories than good ones."

Kyle leaned over and gave me a quick kiss before grabbing another slice of bread to spread mayonnaise on.

"Did Roy have a sense of whether Sam intended to kill Judge Harper or just scare him?" Kyle asked.

"Now there's the really bizarre thing. Sam said he tampered with the judge's brake line as retaliation for sleeping with his mother. He swears he only meant it as a warning to back off. He had no idea the judge was taking a second look at Jennifer Reinhold's murder."

"Well, that's random," Kyle said.

"It really is. The whole thing was so senseless."

Kyle looked up and I could see that he was checking on the girls and the dogs to make sure everyone was okay before he continued his task. He really was going to make an awesome father.

"By the way," he said after assuring himself that everyone was fine, "while I was chatting with Hunter today, he told me Kate is going to be just fine."

"Yeah, Roy told me the same thing. I guess she went over to talk to Sam about tampering with Judge Harper's car, but his neighbor told her that he'd gone over to his mother's. She went there to speak to him, but he wasn't there yet, so Kate decided to have another chat with Martha. During the chat Sam showed up and somehow managed to get her gun."

"She owes you her life."

I began adding slices of ham to the bread Kyle had dressed. "Maybe, but Roy also made it perfectly clear she still believes civilians should stay out of law enforcement business and warned him that if he works with us again she'll report him."

"You're kidding! After everything you did to help her?"

"I know. I should be furious, but somehow I'm not." I began

to distribute the lettuce as Kyle added cheese to the ham. "Kate obviously has a strong opinion about this, and even though I saved her life, she doesn't really know us. I figure we'll just stand back and give her time to settle in. Hopefully there won't be another murder to solve for a long, long time."

Kyle waved at the girls to head in. "That hasn't been the case in the past, but I hope we're entering into a drama-free period in our lives."

Kyle grabbed the soda while I grabbed the chips. He and I weren't a family yet, but, in that moment, I knew exactly how amazing a simple lunch between parents and their children could be.

KATHI DALEY

USA Today bestselling author Kathi Daley lives in beautiful Lake Tahoe with her husband, Ken. When she isn't writing, she likes spending time hiking the miles of desolate trails surrounding her home. She has authored more than seventy-five books in eight series including: Zoe Donovan Cozy Mysteries, Whales and Tails Island Mysteries, Sand and Sea Hawaiian Mysteries, Tj Jensen Paradise Lake Mysteries, Writer's Retreat Southern Seashore Mysteries, Rescue Alaska Paranormal Mysteries, and Seacliff High Teen Mysteries. Find out more about her books at www.kathidaley.com.

**The Tj Jensen Mystery Series
by Kathi Daley**

Henery Press Mystery Books

And finally, before you go...
Here are a few other mysteries
you might enjoy:

MURDER ON A SILVER PLATTER

Shawn Reilly Simmons

A Red Carpet Catering Mystery (#1)

Penelope Sutherland and her Red Carpet Catering company just got their big break as the on-set caterer for an upcoming blockbuster. But when she discovers a dead body outside her house, Penelope finds herself in hot water. Things start to boil over when serious accidents threaten the lives of the cast and crew. And when the film's star, who happens to be Penelope's best friend, is poisoned, the entire production is nearly shut down.

Threats and accusations send Penelope out of the frying pan and into the fire as she struggles to keep her company afloat. Before Penelope can dish up dessert, she must find the killer or she'll be the one served up on a silver platter.

Available at booksellers nationwide and online

Visit www.henerypress.com for details

THE SEMESTER OF OUR DISCONTENT

Cynthia Kuhn

A Lila Maclean Academic Mystery (#1)

English professor Lila Maclean is thrilled about her new job at prestigious Stonedale University, until she finds one of her colleagues dead. She soon learns that everyone, from the chancellor to the detective working the case, believes Lila—or someone she is protecting—may be responsible for the horrific event, so she assigns herself the task of identifying the killer.

Putting her scholarly skills to the test, Lila gathers evidence, but her search is complicated by an unexpected nemesis, a suspicious investigator, and an ominous secret society. Rather than earning an "A" for effort, she receives a threat featuring the mysterious emblem and must act quickly to avoid failing her assignment...and becoming the next victim.

Available at booksellers nationwide and online

Visit www.henerypress.com for details

LIVING THE VIDA LOLA

Melissa Bourbon

A Lola Cruz Mystery (#1)

Meet Lola Cruz, a fiery full-fledged PI at Camacho and Associates. Her first big case? A missing mother who may not want to be found. And to make her already busy life even more complicated, Lola's helping plan her cousin's quinceañera and battling her family and their old-fashioned views on women and careers. She's also reunited with the gorgeous Jack Callaghan, her high school crush whom she shamelessly tailed years ago and photographed doing the horizontal salsa with some other lucky girl.

Lola takes it all in stride, but when the subject of her search ends up dead, she has a lot more to worry about. Soon she finds herself wrapped up in the possibly shady practices of a tattoo parlor, local politics, and someone with serious—maybe deadly—road rage. But Lola is well-equipped to handle these challenges. She's a black-belt in kung fu, and her body isn't her only weapon. She's got smarts, sass, and more tenacity than her Mexican mafioso-wannabe grandfather. A few of her famous margaritas don't hurt, either.

Available at booksellers nationwide and online

Visit www.henerypress.com for details

CROPPED TO DEATH

Christina Freeburn

A Faith Hunter Scrap This Mystery (#1)

Former US Army JAG specialist, Faith Hunter, returns to her West Virginia home to work in her grandmothers' scrapbooking store determined to lead an unassuming life after her adventure abroad turned disaster. But her quiet life unravels when her friend is charged with murder – and Faith inadvertently supplied the evidence. So Faith decides to cut through the scrap and piece together what really happened.

With a sexy prosecutor, a determined homicide detective, a handful of sticky suspects and a crop contest gone bad, Faith quickly realizes if she's not careful, she'll be the next one cropped.

Available at booksellers nationwide and online

Visit www.henerypress.com for details

www.ingramcontent.com/pod-product-compliance
Lightning Source LLC
Chambersburg PA
CBHW070445260626
47161CB00004B/1208